Oria's Enchantment

Sorcerous Moons – Book 5

BY

Jeffe Kennedy

THE TEMPTATION OF POWER

No longer a princess and not yet a queen, the sorceress Oria welcomes the rush of power the ancient mask brings her—though the obsessive connection to it frightens her and alarms her barbarian husband, Lonen. But retreat is not an option. She must wrestle the magic to prevent an annihilating war, even if she must make the ultimate sacrifice.

A WORLD IN FLAMES

If Lonen wants to reclaim his throne—and save his people from destruction—he must return by sunset on the seventh day. What he thought would be a short and simple journey, however, leads them deeper into the mountains—and Oria deeper into the thrall of foul magic. Until he must choose between two terrible paths.

A HEART-WRENCHING CHOICE

Struggling with conflicting loyalties, Oria and Lonen fight to find a way to be together... lest they be separated forever, and their realms go down in flames with them.

Dedication

For Terri Beth Chenault Verrette,
Who accused me of ending the last book "mid-paragraph,"
And who became an insistent voice among many that I finish
this series.

Acknowledgements

Many, many thanks to Nathan Lowell, who asked me every time we talked (and we're both on the SFWA Board of Directors, so it was often) when I was going to finish this series.

Huge thanks, too, to all of the readers who emailed, messaged, tweeted, and mentioned how much they wanted the next book. I'm truly chagrined I made you wait two years for this—and also grateful for your "pestering." Always feel free to do that! Without all of you asking, I might never have made it back around to this tale.

Merci to Melliane for her work behind the scenes—and for sticking with me.

A special thank you to Carien, for an early read and excellent feedback. And for everything else, as usual, *ad infinitum*.

Very special and heartfelt thanks to Kelly Robson, whose daily presence online carried me through some difficult drafting. You always know what book I'm working on—and you always ask how it's going. That means more than I can ever say.

Love—yesterday, today, and always—to David, who shares my days and nights. I wouldn't change a thing, my dear.

Thank you for reading!

Credits
Line and Copy Editor: Rebecca Cremonese
Cover Design: Arel B. Grant, BZN Studio Designs

~ 1 ~

THE MASK HUNG in her awareness like a blinding sun, scorching bright and enticingly hot. Not that the wintry mountain air made her all that cold. Her husband, Lonen, had gone to great lengths to make sure she stayed warm. No, this was like a physical craving. Oria thirsted for more of the golden mask's rich magic, starving for another taste.

With every stride of Lonen's warhorse, Buttercup, with every minute since that morning when she'd held the artifact in her hands, swept under by its immense power, she missed it exponentially more.

Naturally, she wouldn't tell Lonen.

It wouldn't help anything for him to know how deeply the mask affected her. She'd admitted to being frightened by it and that unwise admission had been more than enough. Freshly shaken from the encounter, she'd promised Lonen she wouldn't use the mask by herself. "Fear," however, didn't accurately describe her emotions.

"Greed" would be a better word—and now she deeply regretted that hasty promise. She wanted the mask with a longing unlike anything she'd felt before, except for perhaps during sexplay with Lonen. He had a way of stoking overpowering need in her. Perhaps if they could have actual intercourse, with skin-to-skin contact, that driving desire might be slaked. As it was, despite his inventive alternatives—or, more likely, entirely as a result of those frustrating games of his—their sexual interludes drove all rational sense from her mind, until she could think of nothing but begging for more and more and more.

She wanted the mask like that—but no amount of begging Lonen would work in this case. She had to find another way.

Even now, riding in the cradle of Lonen's arm, cozy in the shadowcat fur cloak, with the startling peaks of the snow-capped mountains rising against the jewel-bright blue sky, she couldn't rest content. The mask mentally tugged at her. After the session with it in the chapel, Lonen had taken the mask from her, holding it suspiciously in gloved hands—and keeping it out of hers. All because she'd lost a bit of time while communing with it, and felt a little ill and disoriented afterward. He flatly refused to give it back, too, and she couldn't match Lonen's physical strength.

Fortunately, she'd managed to persuade him that they needed the magical artifact and he'd agreed to bring it with them. She'd know how to handle it better next time.

There had to be a next time.

She didn't know what extremes she might've gone to if he'd insisted on leaving it behind. Or worse, if he'd walled it up again in that tomb behind stones too heavy for her to budge. Though, if he had gone to such an extreme, she could perhaps have used magic to change the balance of power between them.

She'd barely begun to practice magic in active ways before they fled Bára. Leaving her home—and the deep, ancestral well of sgath magic beneath the walled city—had stripped her of her birthright of power along with her crown. Now the short and overwhelming session with the mask had filled her with such immense reservoirs of sgath magic that she bubbled over with it. She had little experience, and no doubt even less dexterity, at converting passive sgath to active grien to use it as a tool, but she possessed plenty of punch.

Enough to overcome Lonen. Just to take the mask. That's all.

The unfamiliar power tingled in her fingertips, begging to be released, to be exploited…

No. She wouldn't do that. She'd risk harming Lonen, perhaps permanently. She loved him and would never hurt him. And yet…

The mask belonged to *her.* Lonen knew that as well as anyone. He'd taken her to the chapel because he recognized Oria's resemblance to the ancient sorceress depicted in the retablo paintings. It belonged to Oria and her people, not to the barbarian Destrye who'd stolen her ancestress away. Anyone who came between Oria and that mask would suffer just consequences.

The mask whispered to her, full of sweet, heady power she could sense, but that only trickled weakly since she couldn't touch it. Lonen had wrapped the mask in layers of leather, knotted the ties that bound it, and then buried it at the bottom of the saddlebags, which he all but sat on.

When they stopped to eat, however, he might answer the call of nature. While he was off in the woods, she could extract the mask and drink in its magic. It wanted her to. That morning, Oria had only been able to take in a bit, the mask had sat stagnant so long and her sgath portals had been jammed shut with disuse. Recovering from physical starvation had worked that way, too. Her stomach had shrunk so that when she'd gotten the right food, she'd had to eat slowly, to give her system time to recover. But she'd also eaten frequently.

Refilling her empty reserves with sgath again could follow the same pattern.

Lonen, however, distrusted the mask too much. To be fair, she had lost control during that first session, but she knew better now. If she could get to the mask, even only for a few minutes, she'd prove that to him.

"I'd help. I could get the mask out faster than you. I have sharp teeth and sharper claws," Chuffta bragged, not idly.

Oria glanced up to where her Familiar flew overhead, as dazzlingly white as the snow all around them, but with iridescent rainbow shimmers in his scales. The winged lizard looked surprisingly at home in the wintry landscape, so far from his desert habitat. He cocked his head at her, piercing green gaze meeting hers over the downbeat of his translucent leathery wings.

"I look like I belong because I match the snow is all. It's far too cold here. What we need is fire! I could burn the saddlebag and free the mask—it won't melt." He breathed a puff of green fire in demonstration.

"We promised Lonen that neither of us would touch it without him," she reminded Chuffta silently, aware that she'd been perfectly ready to break that promise only a moment ago.

"You promised," he grumbled. *"I didn't promise Lonen anything."*

"Only because he can't hear you like I can. He trusts me to speak for you." And he trusted her to abide by her promise. Her thoughts had gone far down a dark and twisting path. How could she have been plotting to break her word, so soon after giving it?

"Lonen doesn't understand how the mask feels," Chuffta commented, a wistful tone to his mental voice. *"He's only a mind-dead barbarian. He'll never be able to understand."*

"Chuffta!" She stifled a physical gasp of reaction at her Familiar's thoughts, an unpleasant echo of Báran attitudes toward Lonen's people.

"You thought the same thing before," Chuffta complained, but sounded chastened.

"Before I knew better. Now we both *know better."* But Chuffta had a point—that Lonen didn't understand magic. He couldn't. It would be up to her to show him. Just a taste of the mask's power. *"All right, let's do it. I'll suggest that we stop. But no destroying the saddlebags. There's stuff in there that we need."*

"People stuff," he grumbled. *"Derkesthai don't need so much stuff."*

"Lucky you."

"What are you and Chuffta discussing?" Lonen asked, his deep voice a rumble against her back.

She jumped inside her skin, but managed to conceal it by turning her startled and guilty jerk into a wriggle. Leaning against him, reminding herself of the protection that his strong body offered—and the affection and trust that came with it— she tipped her head back to look at her husband. Apparently impervious to the cold, he'd thrown back the furry hood of his cloak, so the chill breeze off the mountain peaks tossed his unruly dark curls, the bright sunlight only emphasizing the glossy blue-black of his hair, the ruggedness of his features, and the granite of his gaze. "How do you always know?" she asked.

He plucked a strand of her long hair that had blown across her face, carefully not touching her skin, and wound it around his finger as he studied her expression. "I don't always know, do I? Only sometimes do I realize you must be, and mostly from the way he behaves." Lonen jerked his chin at Chuffta, who'd surged forward to soar along the edge of a precipice, taking advantage of the rising thermals stirred from the valleys by the intense sun. "He looks at you, flies closer, breathes flame sometimes." Lonen raised his brows in question.

"He likes to brag," Oria explained.

"But you, your expression and manner don't often reveal much." His voice lowered, a certain suspicion in it.

"That was part of my training, as a member of the royal family and the priestess they expected me to become. I worked very hard to learn to compose myself so as not to reveal emotion."

"You're very good at it. Which worries me. You're acting strangely now."

"Now?" She suspected where he was going with this and asked the question more as a delaying tactic. Lonen saw through her far better than he pretended.

"Since this morning and your encounter with that … thing."

His scarred eye twitched, and she lifted a gloved hand to his face, the scarlet velvet a startling contrast to his brown skin, and smoothed the nap over that brow. The newer scar over the old one, both crossing his eye above and below, pulled pink and new, and he sometimes rubbed it as if it pained him, though her barbarian warrior wasn't one to complain. If only she could truly touch him.

"I'm still me," she said, giving him a reassuring smile. "And I'm feeling so much better now. Especially with the magic from Tania's mask." She'd decided to call her unnamed ancestress after a long-lost aunt. If only she could persuade him to let her keep the mask on her person… "I'm excited to try again since the mask will—"

"Will stay in the saddlebags for now," he cut her off, narrowing his gaze on her face.

Annoyed, she turned away so he wouldn't see it in her,

how much she wanted—*needed*—just another small taste. "I have to learn to work with it if we're to have a hope of saving Dru from Yar and the Trom."

"Yes, well," he replied, sounding drily amused but also resolved, "winning that war shouldn't be an issue in the next few hours, and I want you to have some distance from that thing before you go near it again."

"It's mine, Lonen," she replied tightly, curling her velvet-clad fingers against the urge to claw him. "Your ancestor may have taken Tania captive and bred children on her, but she was of *my* people, not yours."

"Oh?" He replied with lethal softness. "And here I recall a vow when you married me that you'd be my wife and Queen of the Destrye, that you would take Dru as your responsibility and the people as your own."

Curse his clever tongue.

"He does have a point," Chuffta said, sounding as chastened as she felt.

"Only partially." Speaking aloud, she said, "As your brothers and numerous other Destrye, including your Priest of Arill, have noted, I am *not* Queen of Dru and won't be unless we're married according to *your* goddess."

"According to *your* temple, your ways, and the evidence of my own senses," he shot back immediately, "the bond between us was magically forged and cannot be broken."

She opened her mouth with a vague thought of arguing, but the tightening of his arms around her stopped her words in her throat.

"Don't try to deny that, sorceress," he murmured in her ear, "because even this mind-dead barbarian can sense magic at that level."

"I didn't know you could sense the magic of the marriage

bond so strongly," she said aloud. Had he told her that? She didn't think so. How odd.

"You're like a burning sun inside me, Oria," he murmured in her ear, his lips so close only the veil of her hair prevented contact.

With him so near, his emotions flew into her like arrows, and she narrowed her magic portals to control the onslaught. Love, desire, fear, worry… and hope balancing the razor edge of despair. Lonen was a man of passionate feelings, which he projected with the same exuberant force as his personality, and it could be too much for her to bear, on so many levels.

"It doesn't matter what my brothers or the priests say," he continued with grim resolve, "you're wedded so tightly to my soul I imagine you'll be there after this body is gone and blown to ash in the wind."

She shivered at the images. Too many of them too similar to her own thoughts.

"But," he continued in a more cheerful tone, thankfully giving her a bit more room, "their objections won't matter much longer because when we return, we'll be wed under Arill's hand as well. Then there will be no doubts."

"Do you think your mother will be willing to journey back with us and sponsor the marriage?" Oria did have doubts. Many of them.

"Yes." He said it with finality, though she wondered how he planned to convince this former queen who lived in some sort of exile or hermitage, far from her family and the forests of Dru. It had never been clear to Oria why his mother lived so far from the center of Destrye government and Lonen had ducked answering her questions. "I wouldn't be dragging you on this journey otherwise," he added, after a moment.

"I thought you brought me along because you wanted to

show me Odymesen's chapel, because you thought the magic there might help me, and it did." She didn't need to remind either of them that they'd both feared for her safety in the palace without him there to protect her.

"True. I hope I don't regret that."

"If you're that concerned," she replied, stung, "it seems unwise to marry me any more than you already have."

His strong arm slid around her waist, pulling her back against him, though she remained stiff. "I don't regret finding magic for you, beloved Oria," he said quietly. "Only that the nature of what we found might jeopardize your wellbeing."

"It won't," she answered. "You have to trust me there."

Making a noncommittal sound, he didn't offer any guarantee. Silence fell between them, fraught with the argument neither of them wanted to continue.

"How long to your mother's abode?" she finally asked.

"We'll be there tonight. A day to persuade her, two days' journey back, and we'll return to the temple and Arill City in plenty of time."

"Your brother can have you declared dead seven days from when he issued the challenge—that's only two days of leeway," she worried.

"Two days we won't need," Lonen replied, as carelessly and confidently optimistic as ever. "Once that's done, we can end this ridiculous infighting with my family and face our true enemy."

"Our wedding won't guarantee your victory in the duel against Nolan for the throne," she felt compelled to point out.

"With my powerful sorceress wife as my second?" He made a scoffing sound. "I cannot lose."

If she could wield her magic effectively. "All the more reason for me to practice with the mask."

"Later, Oria." He nearly growled her name, punctuating it with finality. "You'll mess with that thing in small doses or I'll melt it in the nearest campfire."

The threat sent a pang of panic through her. "Chuffta says it can't be melted."

"Does he now?" Lonen sounded so interested that she realized she'd revealed too much, that he now knew she and her Familiar had been discussing the magical artifact Lonen already mistrusted so greatly. "I wouldn't be so sure," he continued when she didn't reply. "The Destrye have long since mastered the art of metal work of all kinds. We no doubt have a kiln that will do the job."

"You wouldn't."

"I absolutely would. Make no mistake, Oria—I will destroy that thing rather than lose you to it."

She wanted to laugh—even tried to—but made a strained sound instead, so stricken was she by the panic that he'd carry out that threat and she'd lose the mask forever. "You won't lose me to it," she replied, loading her tone with scorn to cover the urge to beg him to give it to her. "It's a tool, nothing more."

"Good." He spoke the word shortly, nearly a grunt. "Then, as with all dangerous tools, you will learn to employ this one carefully and gradually—and under my supervision."

She set her teeth, well past annoyed with him, the fury in her heart burning as bright as any kiln. That did it. He didn't have authority over her. He could take his "supervision" and—

"Oria—do I have your agreement?"

"Fine, yes."

"Good. Thank you, love."

"Do we have time for a rest break?" she asked as smoothly as she could. "I need to visit the woods."

"Of course. You have only to say." Responding to subtle signals, Buttercup eased to a stop. Lonen swung down, offering his hands to help her down, smiling with affection. It might be enough to make her feel guilty for what she was about to do, but not quite. "Can you make it through the snow?" he asked.

"Yes." She gave him a dazzling smile, knowing how it affected him; the lazy curl of desire emanating from him warming her. Chuffta followed above as she tromped through the snow, then he perched on a branch to guard her while she did her business. *Is Lonen still with Buttercup?* she asked him.

He swiveled his head on his long mobile neck, snaking it for the best angle between the interlacing bare branches. *Yes. He's getting something out of the saddlebags.*

Couldn't be the mask. Unless he was making good on his threat to get rid of it. Hurrying, she clambered back through the deep snow. It had a crunchy layer on the top, but the snow was fluffy beneath, so she sank to her knees in places. Good thing she had the tall boots and fur-lined stockings.

"Hungry?" Lonen asked as she reached firmer ground of the trail. He held out a packet of seeds, dried fruit, and buttery grains—thoughtfully provided just for her. For his part, he chewed on some dried meat.

"Thank you." She took it, feeling chagrined at his thoughtfulness. But not enough to go back on her plan. He started to pack things away again. "I can do that," she offered. "If you need to visit the woods, too."

He grinned for her euphemism, and ran a hand down her arm over the cloak. "Do the woods need more visitors?" he teased.

"You know what I mean," she replied, more primly than she might have if she hadn't been mentally urging him to go, afraid that if he delayed he'd see through her subterfuge.

Hesitating, he frowned a little. "I guess I do feel the need after all. Will you be all right waiting for me?"

"Of course," she said brightly, though a sick feeling wormed in her gut. Had she somehow pushed his will? She'd never been able to do that before, but…

"I'll be right back, love," he promised, and cupped her head to kiss her through the furry cloak on the crown of her head.

Oria watched him go, tension mounting. Moving so Buttercup stood between her and where Lonen had gone, she scrabbled through the open pack, hoping fervently that Lonen had put the mask in that one. Chuffta landed on Buttercup's saddle, craning his sinuous neck to see. Remaining on alert as Lonen had signaled the warhorse to do, Buttercup ignored them and watched the surroundings.

"Hurry!"

"Is Lonen already coming back?"

"No, but hurry anyway."

With a gusty breath of relief, she closed her fingers around the oddly shaped bundle that was Tania's mask, hard metal within layers of leather, the potent magic of the ancient sorceress singing its siren call of sweet, pure power.

"Yesss," Chuffta hissed with metal glee. *"Hurryhurryhurry."*

Her fingers shook, fumbling at the tight leather knots, and she impatiently yanked off her glove with her teeth. The cold air and frozen hard sinew cut into her skin, and she was just about to let Chuffta cut it apart when the knot gave. Tossing the sinews and wrapping to the snow, Oria grasped the smooth gold metal fashioned to look like a blank, eyeless face.

As it had before, the magic grabbed at her, but she wrangled it this time, not letting it pull her under. Instead she inhaled, absorbed, consumed, gorging on the feast of it.

So much gorgeous sgath. Sustaining. Nourishing. Overwhelming.

She began to suffocate under the force of it, to choke on the sheer purity of it. It bloated her, stretching her skin to bursting, her magic portals springing leaks. Swirling, she drowned in the rush of it.

"Oria! Arill take you, come out of it!" Lonen roared in her face, his grip bruising her arms as he shook her.

The sun scorched her vision, the blue sky and white snow all too bright. She put a hand up to cover her eyes and her fingers skidded wet and sticky with blood, sharp pain spiking.

"I could throttle you for this," Lonen grated out.

"What happened—where are you?" she asked Chuffta.

"I'm here." Her Familiar sounded uncharacteristically meek and chastened. *"Lonen told me to get lost. He's mad at me, too."*

"Me, Oria," Lonen said with a snarl. "Talk to me, not him. What in Arill's name made you break your promise?"

"Extracted under duress!" she fired back. "You do not order me, Destrye."

"In this I do. That cursed thing nearly killed you this time."

"I almost had it. I just have to learn to handle the mask so that—"

"Look at your hands." He glared at her with fury—but also fear and worry, enough to give her pause.

She looked, shocked to find her hands covered in blood, fresh and wet over caked and brown. Now that she'd regained awareness, her body throbbed with pain, her neck stiff and hair sticky. She put a hand to her ear, fingers coming away with more blood.

"You were bleeding out of your ears, eyes, nose, and mouth," Lonen informed her. "Even after I got that thing out of your grip—which ripped the skin off your hands, by the way—you wouldn't come out of the trance. You weren't breathing, Oria. Explain to me how that is *learning to handle it!*" His voice climbed to a shout at the end, his face wild.

But it was the sheer panic flowing from him that penetrated her indignation. Lonen so rarely showed fear or worried about much at all. Even when any rational person would. She'd managed to terrify her perpetual optimist, a warrior so strong nothing frightened him.

"I'm sorry," she said, infusing the words with all the sincere regret she could muster. "I was foolish and I won't do it again."

He held her still, looking a bit crazed as he searched her face, then crushed her to him. "I can't lose you, Oria. It would break me as nothing else could."

"I promise I won't do it again," she said against him, meaning it with all her heart. Still, she mentally asked Chuffta the question, *"Did he try to destroy the mask?"*

"No. It's in the snow where he threw it."

Good. Now to make sure Lonen agreed to wrap it up again and bring it with them.

~ 2 ~

"ABSOLUTELY NOT." LONEN folded his arms, staring Oria down. She'd scrubbed all the blood off with snow, giving her face a pink-cheeked glow, her bright copper eyes snapping at him.

Her physical injuries had turned out to be minor, which would be a good thing except that she'd rebounded so quickly. And now she crackled with magic, her copper hair lifting in the unseen currents of it as she faced him, a stubborn look on her lovely face. She might be small and delicate in build, but the magic snarling around her made him cautious. He didn't think she'd use that magic to attack him. Then again, he hadn't thought she'd break her promise either.

"I'll keep the mask with me," she repeated.

"You're lucky I've agreed to wrap it up again and stow it in the bags." He finished that wrapping, hating the metallic glint of the thing with every fiber of his being.

Oria stepped close, as if to snatch it from him, and he held it out of her reach. She had too much pride to jump for it, but the air between them thickened, almost seeming to produce sparks from nothing.

"Don't do it, Oria," he said softly, though he didn't know how he'd stop her if she did.

"I'm not doing anything," she replied evenly.

Ha to that. "I can feel you inside me," he reminded her. "Your magic snarling, sizzling. Would you strike me down, love? Because of that mask?"

"Because you're not my lord and master, barbarian," she replied with heat. "I'm not a helpless, captive Báran bride and you'd do well to remember that."

As if he could ever forget. It made him want to laugh, so he let it out, a hearty release that had her blinking at him in shock. "Oh, my copper-haired beauty, I am more like to forget my own name than the power of the witch I brought home from war and installed in my bed." He deliberately dropped his voice as he said it, to remind her of what they shared together. It worked, too, her anger turning into another kind of heat. "Nor do I forget how to tame her," he added, not above goading her, especially if it distracted her.

"Not fair," she hissed at him, clenching her small fists by her sides. "Don't you dare bring sex into this."

"You're the one who brought it up," he replied with an easy smile, picturing her naked, tied up and tossed over his shoulder, hoping she'd pluck the image from his mind. She must have, because she made an incoherent sound of frustration, with a nicely sensual edge to it. Working quickly, he secured the last knot and stowed the mask deeply in the saddlebag, wedging in everything he could fit on top of it. Not that he'd leave her alone with it again. "Ready to go?" he asked, turning his back to her.

Without waiting for her response, he lifted her onto Buttercup's back, then swung up behind her. They practiced the maneuver so often that they immediately and smoothly nestled together. At least their bodies were in complete harmony. Even blisteringly angry with him, Oria leaned into him without hesitation.

"How are you feeling?" he asked.

"Perfectly fine," she retorted, so fast he'd know it for the lie that it was even if he couldn't see the shadows under her eyes, through her waxy, translucent skin, and the too-glassy look in her eyes. She still sparked with jittering energy, the way some warriors did when they fought too long on too little sleep: running on purely manic energy that eventually buried them.

Oria had told him early on that her peculiar nature made her oversensitive. Without a way to bleed off magical energy, it crackled and fried inside her, hollowing her out into exhaustion. Well, he might not know magic, but he knew how to help her relax. He slipped a hand inside her cloak, cupping the luscious globe of her breast—then pinched the nipple that eagerly rose to his touch.

"My tame witch," he murmured in her ear when she gasped. "You are more than fine."

"I'm not a witch," she replied tightly, but she also pressed her breast into his hand, though perhaps unaware of it—or of how she pushed her tight little bottom against his crotch.

"You admitted it last night. Remember?"

"Lonen…" She spoke his name on a helpless breath, her body growing hotter against him. Oh yes, she remembered, just as he did.

"You said you were my tame witch because you need this." She wore layers of skirts and petticoats, but he knew his way through them. Giving Buttercup the signal to continue on, Lonen secured the reins to drape loosely and slipped his other hand to the thin layer of fine cloth between her spread thighs. The fur-lined stockings tied high on her legs kept her plenty warm, as did all the heavy layers, but very little shielded her open sex. She burned hot and wet against his hand as he cupped her mound, her sweetly plump sex filling his palm.

She moaned and sagged against him. "Lonen… please," she said on a sighing mewl of pleasure. She put her gloved hand over his, but didn't pull his hand away from her intimate flesh, instead rocking her hips against the light pressure—and consequently against his trapped and turgid cock. "Anyone could see," Oria said, though she had her eyes closed, shivering with arousal.

He laughed, not heartily this time, hearing the huskiness of desire in it, and working his fingers against her, knowing exactly how she liked it. "There's leagues of empty landscape all around with no one to see or hear. You could scream your pleasure if you like," he suggested. He loved it when she forgot herself enough in desire to sob his name like a prayer.

"I won't." But the words came out uncertain as she panted, squirming against his pinning hand.

"You did last night," he crooned into her ear. "Over and over. You begged me."

She didn't reply. Even Oria couldn't argue with that truth. He'd driven her wild, driven them both into a frenzy. She'd worn the crimson velvet gloves and he used his leather ones to torment every part of her, determined not to leave even so much as a fingertip of skin that he hadn't thoroughly possessed. Those firelit memories swamped him, lurid and sensual, both of them naked but for the gloves they each wore, how he'd stared into her eyes as he used his leather-covered fingers to penetrate her. How she'd come apart, calling his name.

With a sharp cry she barely stifled, she came against his hand, a wrenching convulsion that had her arching, thighs tensing as she shuddered helplessly. He held her through it, pushing her harder and higher, murmuring wicked things in her ear, until she sagged against him, boneless and unresisting.

"That's better," he said softly, kissing her hair. Clean now, and hot from the sun, it tasted sweet.

"What is?" she asked, her voice vague.

"You needed to relax."

"You can't use sex to handle me, Lonen," she said, though she sounded more sleepy than anything, languid in his arms.

"You're welcome to use the same techniques on me. 'Tis a time-honored tradition between lovers." He shifted behind her, adjusting the hard thrust of his cock, quite painful now that he wasn't distracted. "Though perhaps not now."

"Still sore?" she asked, sounding entirely unsympathetic, even giggling softly.

"Yes, witch." It wasn't funny at all to the possessor of the cock rubbed raw by her gloves. "Lesson learned that though velvet gloves seem soft, the eventual chafing puts the lie to that."

Her giggles rang out in girlishly light, even giddy notes, doing a great deal to lighten his own heart. "There was a definite resemblance in color," she pointed out pertly.

"Sure, laugh," he grumbled. "It's already less painful. To-night you'll be making it up to me."

"Not at your mother's house," she said without missing a beat.

"My mother did conceive and bear four children," he commented, teasing her. "I expect she knows what people get up to in bed."

"Yes, but she doesn't need us doing that sort of thing under her roof," she answered in a prim tone. "I'd like to make a good impression."

"Don't worry about that," he said. He must've sounded gruff because she leaned back to look at him in that assessing way that meant she read his thoughts. He offered her a smile, though it felt false even to himself. No need to get into ancient history. "To answer your earlier question, my mother *will* agree to sponsor our marriage to the temple, but she won't be doing it because of any impression you make. This has nothing to do with you and everything to do with me."

"I don't understand." Oria frowned, then yawned.

"No, I imagine not. But you'll see." He set his jaw and lifted his gaze to the peaks ahead. "She owes me."

Oria fell asleep soon after that. She would have done so long before, if that Arill-cursed mask hadn't had her so obsessed. The magic infusion had helped her immensely, but Oria had a long recovery ahead of her and she needed rest to heal her emaciated body as much as she needed the right food and nourishing magic.

He'd regret having kept her awake so much of the night with their lovemaking, if that too didn't have such a salutary effect on her. She might not even be aware of how much that affected her, both energizing and soothing her. Oria might make acerbic comments about him controlling her access to the mask and how she used her magic, but he'd begun to wonder if he didn't have a larger role to play in her sorcery than either of them had imagined.

She sighed in her sleep, snuggling against him with all the trust she'd withheld when awake and angry with him. Her lovely profile stood out in pale contrast to the shining copper of her hair, fiery in the sunlight and framed in the dappled shadowcat fur so perfect for showcasing her exotic beauty. In sleep she seemed all soft and fragile woman, with little evidence of the immensely powerful sorcery that burned within her. It consumed her, that magic, like a fever thinning her skin—and affecting her mind with delirium.

He fervently wished he hadn't given in to Oria's wheedling

that led to unearthing the mask from the tomb. Perhaps she'd been right to chide him for being superstitious about the old prohibitions against violating tombs, but often those warnings that seemed baseless contained dire truths. If he hadn't been so afraid for Oria, so worried that she'd die without access to the magic of Odymesen's sorceress wife, he would've been able to resist what he *knew* was a bad idea. But he'd given in, and the mask did seem to at least provide Oria with the magic she needed to survive. He'd also studied the inscriptions on the tomb of that ancient pair.

And he hadn't told Oria all of it.

Odymesen had loved his sorceress wife, yes, a woman of Oria's people, captured in war and brought back to the forests of Dru. She'd lived a long life among them—unlike her sister sorceresses who'd languished and died, much as Oria had been on the way to doing—and she'd brought great gifts to the Destrye during that lifetime. But the inscriptions also warned that Odymesen had been pressed to serve as guardian to those gifts, that his sorceress's magic could turn dark and deadly.

In the end, he'd killed her with his own hands, to stop her from some terrible, unnamed destruction. Looking at his lovely Oria, sleeping so trustingly in his arms, Lonen couldn't imagine harming her. And yet…

And yet he'd felt the magic of that mask in her. It snarled in her voice, like another being entirely, and fueled a fury not native to her gentle nature. For a few moments, at the height of her rage, he'd been afraid of her. Her magic had been a palpable threat, like a coiled serpent poised to strike him down. The mask gave her the fuel for her sorcerous abilities, but it also somehow influenced how she used them. Perhaps even corrupting her will.

The way she'd looked, collapsed in the snow, clutching

that mask even as her blood poured down her unconscious face… He'd remember that gut-watering sight until the day he died.

Chuffta returned from his forays, swooping and circling overhead. Oria's Familiar always showed discretion that way, giving them privacy for sexual intimacy—though not for much else. The derkesthai Familiar had helped Oria get the mask, encouraged her somehow, Lonen felt sure. Chuffta gave him a long, almost speculative look as he slowed his circling, his green eyes glittering bright. Not a reassuring expression at all.

While he and Chuffta had established a friendly relationship, Lonen harbored no illusions that the derkesthai's loyalty belonged to anyone but Oria. He acted in her best interests, but Chuffta was also young and easily swayed by shiny and interesting things, like fire. Or powerful magical artifacts. Chuffta had been as attracted to the mask as Oria was—which meant Lonen could find himself fighting the pair of them.

Wonderful. He possessed no magic, had no Familiar of his own, unless you counted Buttercup, which he didn't. The warhorse, while uncommonly intelligent and certainly powerful, wasn't a magical companion on par with the derkesthai. He and the horse had only brute strength, stamina, and fighting excellence on their side of the arsenal. Yes, Buttercup understood him with near perfect communication, but not in the same way.

Not enough to counter sorcery like he'd seen the Báran war mages employ. Hopefully he worried unnecessarily about a battle that would never come to pass.

Still, no matter that Oria teased him about his sunny optimism, Lonen had a hard time seeing how this would turn out well. For the time being though, he'd do his best to savor the moment. His beautiful—and healing—bride asleep in his arms, the scent of pine forest and fresh snow, the hot glance of the sun on his face.

All of them safe and well, if only for the space of an afternoon.

~ 3 ~

"O RIA."

The sound of her name pulled her from deep sleep and strange dreams. Not nightmares for once, but still odd visions of people and lands she didn't recognize. She'd been dancing around a fire to the throbbing beat of huge copper-clad drums, the hammered metal glinting with rose-gold light. Scantily clad, she'd felt sleek and sinuous, moving her body to the powerful beat while her husband watched, desire and fear in his dark eyes. He'd gripped the arms of his throne with powerful hands as the magic rose in her, a fire in her blood that drowned out all else.

The crown of Dru rested on his head, the metal leaves of the wreath twined through his thick dark curls, threads of silver at his temples and in his long beard. Her husband. Her king.

With the wrong face. Not Lonen, but some other Destrye king.

She blinked at him in drowsy confusion, Lonen's face like and unlike the man in her dream. The same broad cheekbones, the dark hair and beard, the same powerful mien of the Destrye warriors that even the illustrations back in Bára had shown more or less accurately.

The eyes, though, they were different. Lonen's were a

deep granite gray, with lush black lashes that would be feminine on a softer visage. They held love without fear—and a delighted sparkle. Above his beard, his mouth curved in a mischievous smile of anticipation.

She'd fallen in love with him because of his humor. Well, for many reasons, but first for that. Even when the Destrye suffered terrible defeat in Bára, when he'd faced horrors monstrous enough to leave his skin ashen and his eyes dark as pits, he'd been able to laugh—and make her laugh in turn. As always unable to resist that impish charm in him, she smiled back. "What has you looking like the derkesthai that devoured a nest of eggs?"

"*I only did that once,*" Chuffta mentally sniffed in offense. "*And I was new to Bára.*"

"You ate the high priestess's clutch of prized songbirds," she reminded Chuffta aloud, for Lonen's benefit, keeping the amusement out of her tone though she grinned at Lonen.

"He did?" Lonen grinned, too, and flicked a glance at the circling Familiar. "Chuffta, man—bad form."

"*I didn't know!*" he complained, then added, "*but they didn't taste like prized anything. More important, there's something very exciting just ahead.*"

"Chuffta says there's something interesting ahead?"

Lonen scowled. "Did he spoil the surprise?"

"No. He wouldn't." Just to be sure, she mentally reminded Chuffta not to tell her. He sent her a scornful, wordless thought in reply. She levered herself up, her body protesting and unexpectedly stiff. "I must've slept a long time," she noted, realizing she'd slipped down all but horizontal in Lonen's firm hold.

"Half the day," Lonen agreed, nodding his chin at the sun, which now lowered in the sky ahead of them. Afternoon then, and not morning at all anymore. He raised a challenging brow at her exclamation of dismay. "You needed the rest."

Apparently, but how thoughtless of her. "But you must be starving, and you haven't had a break from riding all this time." Then she caught herself, remembering what happened the last time she encouraged him to take a break.

He lowered his brows, giving her a patient look. "Oria, my love, I've been glued to the saddle without food or rest for far longer than this on campaigns. I hardly noticed."

She rolled her eyes at him, relieved that he wasn't going to castigate her further for what she'd done. "So stalwart and tough, my Destrye warrior."

"I'm glad you finally recognize this truth," he replied solemnly, then grinned when she made a huff of exasperation. "Look." He pointed. "Watch through those trees there."

Peering along the line of his blunt finger, she scanned the forest lining the path. Now that she'd become accustomed to the extraordinary sight of so many trees, tall and dense, covering the landscape in numbers as great as the grains of sand at Bára, she found the forest somewhat frustrating and claustrophobic. You couldn't see anything *but* trees. Their ranks of thick trunks bordered the paths, soaring above on all sides and carving the sky into small pieces. Only when they came to one of the great precipices could she see any distance.

She'd opened her mouth to accuse him of making sport of her when she caught a glimpse of another color between the rows and columns of black trunks and snow-covered ground and branches. There.

Blue.

A blue so vast and bright it reflected like another sky full of sunlight. Like nothing she'd ever seen. Straining her eyes, she searched for another glimpse... Then caught her breath with a joyous wrench of utter shock.

Buttercup had rounded a bend and the vista opened up before them. The forest fell away to either side, the path they followed snaking down a steep hillside, the valley below filled entirely with water.

More water than she'd ever seen in her entire life. More than she'd been able to imagine existed.

"Is it the ocean?" she breathed in wonder.

Lonen laughed, then kissed her hair in apology. "No, my desert lady. It's but a lake. Lake Scandamalion. Not as large as the ones we once had, but the largest that's left—that we know of."

She set aside the wincing guilt that it had been her people who drained the lakes of Dru dry, sucking away the water through tunnels and over time. Hoarding and squandering it, killing the Destrye by slow degrees. "Can we swim in it?" she asked, remembering how Lonen had promised her that.

They'd swum in the water at the oasis—well, he'd swum and she'd waded and floated—but that was nothing compared to the vastness of this lake. A vibration of amusement rumbled in him, though Lonen managed not to laugh out loud this time. Wrapping an arm around her waist and snugging her against him, he pointed toward the hills sloping down toward the water, tracing the line for her while Buttercup stood obediently still.

"See how the snow goes all the way to the water? The lake isn't frozen, but it is snowmelt water—which means it's bitterly cold. You could swim in it—and some like to test themselves that way—but I don't think you would enjoy it."

"No," she agreed fervently, trying to imagine what that might feel like. Back in Bára they'd used ice in drinks, and to freeze fruit sherbets, but it had melted so quickly in the fierce heat that the experience of chill had been fleeting. To immerse in it…

As they watched, Chuffta's small white form soared over the brilliant blue of the lake. Then he folded his wings and dove, spearing into the water.

"Chuffta, no!" she cried.

"*Cold!*" he shouted in her mind, his tone exhilarated. "*There's huge fish in here, too.*"

She groaned, shaking her head, and Lonen laughed, urging Buttercup down the switchback path and taking up the reins again. For the most part Buttercup's thoughts reflected the disciplined stoicism of an impeccably trained warhorse, but just then his mind jumped with excitement at the sight of the lake and the tricky, snow-covered path to it. The horse didn't articulate his thoughts with the clear intelligence that Chuffta did, but he was smarter than many other animals. It always interested her that Lonen seemed to know when Buttercup needed a guiding hand on the reins and when he could be trusted to behave well.

Probably a reflection of Lonen's intuitive nature, which he also employed to gentle her and coax her into behaving well, her body leaping eagerly to his caresses, as well trained as his warhorse and hunting dogs. Thinking of which, she suddenly realized she hadn't thought about craving contact with the mask since she'd awakened. She couldn't decide how she felt about that.

It might be the cowardly choice, but at least for the moment, she decided not to think about it at all.

Lonen regaled her with tales of expeditions to the lake in his youth—a far more carefree era for Dru—and plans to repair and extend the aqueduct network in spring, to bring water to the fields lower down. Neither of them mentioned what had happened to the previous aqueduct the Destrye had labored so hard to build a few short months before. The burn scars along the lakeshore where the wooden structures had been were clearly visible a short distance away. The Trom had burnt them with vicious thoroughness, a maneuver intended only to harm Dru, as Oria's brother Yar, Bára, and Bára's sister cities gained nothing from the move. It wasn't as if the water the Destrye used came out of Báran mouths.

Or did it?

"The tunnels Nolan traveled in, from the lake beneath Bára back to Dru," she wondered, "could they extend to here?"

Lonen halted Buttercup at the water's edge and swung down, holding his arms up for her. "I've thought about that," he replied. Of course he had. Lonen seemed to think of everything far before she did. Bracing herself on his strong forearms, she swung her leg over and he lifted her down as if she weighed nothing. He set her on her feet, but held her there, hands on her waist, a thoughtful expression in his eyes. "I don't think so. Nolan said the tunnels ended north of Arill City, in a region that used to have numerous prairie lakes. For the tunnels to extend all this way, they'd have to travel beneath most of Dru—and go through the granite bedrock of these mountains. Could the Báran sorcerers accomplish such a great feat?"

"I don't know," she admitted. Her knowledge of what the Báran men, even her own father and brothers, could do with their powerful grien magic was woefully thin and riddled with gaping holes. "I didn't know about the tunnels to begin with, or the underground lake beneath the city, until Nolan told us. Before that I would've said no, it couldn't be done, but now I'm not so certain…"

"Could *you* do it, do you think?" He studied her, asking the question in an almost idle tone, but with a certain intensity beneath.

"As a woman, I'm not supposed to be able to wield grien magic at all," she pointed out.

"But we both know you can. Now that you have a store of sgath again, you can maybe channel it into grien, like you did before."

She began to follow his line of thinking. "You want me to bore tunnels through bedrock, to carry water down to the fields. Then the Trom dragons will have nothing to burn."

"It's an ideal solution." His gaze wandered over her face. "If the cost isn't too high."

"With access to the mask, and *practice*," she emphasized, "I should be able to filter the wild magic indefinitely, ordering it into sgath. After that, it would only take time to gradually wear away the rock, I'd think."

He nodded, more confirming something to himself. "Something to consider."

"No sense considering it if you won't let me have the mask." She raised her brows at him, giving him a cold look to make certain he knew she hadn't forgiven him taking control of that.

"I did say we'd have to factor the cost." His hands tightened on her waist, the scar over his eye twisting with a slight tic. "It's not worth your life. Or sanity."

Arrested, she stared at him a moment. "I doubt the stakes are so high. I feel fine."

"I don't know about that." He let her go and turned to survey the lake. "Next summer, when the weather warms, we can come back and you can swim to your heart's content."

"That won't happen if Nolan kills you in a duel for the throne."

"Then I'll have to win."

"And even then, it won't happen unless we can defeat Yar."

"Then we'll do that, too."

"You're so bloody optimistic," she grumbled.

"A good balance for my pretty pessimist." He grinned at her. "See what a great team we make?"

"I see that you deliberately changed the subject."

"Absolutely. Look—Chuffta caught a fish."

"Oh no—Chuffta, let the poor thing go!"

"A big fish! I caught it myself. It's very heavy though." Even his thoughts sounded labored as he flew low over the water toward them, the silvery fish twice the size of Chuffta's body dangling—and flapping, and writhing—in his talons. *"It wants to get away, but it won't. Mine."*

"Let it go. It'll die out of water," she called.

"Yes, it will," Lonen agreed, clapping his hands together. "And will make for fine eating. Good work, Chuffta man."

Chuffta made it to shore and landed heavily, pinning the fish with talons and spread wings, while Lonen grabbed a fist-sized rock and dispatched the fish. Gorge rising, Oria turned away, focusing on the deceptively peaceful and lovely scenery.

"We have food," she pointed out, not looking, though the predatory glee of Chuffta's thoughts and the pleased anticipation of Lonen's kept her apprised of their actions. Both meat-eaters, the pair of them at least shared that hunter's excitement in the catch. At least the fish didn't have emotions, not that she could sense. This was, no doubt, why the magic-users of Bára had been vegetarians for generations. Though her brother Yar had killed human beings without seeming at all affected by it.

"We have some food, yes, but we don't have a fresh stardew," Lonen replied. "Here Chuffta, keep your snout clear of my knife or I'll nick you. The entrails are all yours once I get them out. More important," he said to Oria, "this will make a fine gift for my mother, and should go a long way toward putting her in the right frame of mind."

"And what is the right frame of mind?" Oria muttered the question mostly to herself.

"Generous," Lonen answered, in the same tone.

She wandered along the lakeshore, moving away from the impromptu slaughter—and Chuffta's carnivorous satisfaction. Of course she'd always fed him meat of various kinds, as that was his nature, but in Bára his meals had been delivered in innocuous bites arranged on platters. He'd only started killing for food since they left Bára, with the exception of his occasional youthful lapse. It shouldn't bother her, as she'd been the one to put him in this position. But the predatory glee in him felt something like the vicious killing rages of the Trom dragons.

"The dragons don't eat their kill," Chuffta said with implacable logic. *"They only burn and destroy. Totally different."*

She sent him an affectionate thought, tucking her doubt where he couldn't sense it. Was this how Lonen felt about her—this wary uncertainty? She loved Chuffta without reservation, but the glimpses of the monstrous in him unsettled her. Squatting down, she pulled off her glove and dipped her fingers in the water, startling a little at the biting chill. No wonder Lonen had laughed at her for suggesting they swim. Determinedly she sunk her hand in the water to the wrist, holding it there. If the fire-loving Chuffta could stand to immerse in it, she could take that much discomfort.

She sensed his approach before she heard him. For a big man, he had a habitual warrior's stealth. Lonen crouched beside her, saying nothing for a moment. "Is this a sorceress thing?" he finally asked, quietly, as if taking care not to disturb her.

Glancing at him, she took him in, so robust and in his element here. Without the responsibilities of kingship, he'd relaxed. The chill breeze had his cheeks rosy over the dark beard, and his gray eyes sparkled with spirit. Her hand had gone numb—so interesting—so she lifted it out of the water and shook the droplets off. The cold had made her pale skin even whiter, and the veins stood out blue. "Just testing what I can withstand."

"I think you've passed plenty of tests of strength of will," he noted with a wry smile.

"Have I?" She wiggled her fingers, which felt stiff and not like her own. "This isn't that difficult, once you get over the initial shock—it just goes numb."

He considered her, gaze thoughtful. "It's the easiest death, the Destrye say, to freeze. Some commit suicide that way—going off into the winter. They say that once you get cold enough, you start to feel warm and sleepy. You fall asleep and…" He tipped his head, studying her. "Never wake up again."

A wordless silence fell between them and she wasn't quite sure what they were saying to each other in this odd conversation.

"I have the fish packed up in snow," he finally said, "but if we want it to be fresh, we should leave soon. Plus the sun is going down and it will be getting dark, which brings predators I'd rather not face without a bigger force than ours. If you're ready."

Standing and pulling on her glove again, she nodded.

$$\sim 4 \sim$$

ORIA WAS OMINOUSLY silent. Of course, she tended to be a quiet person, expressing her restless curiosity in movement rather than volubility. Though she'd told him stories about her difficulties in Bára, about not being able to meditate or exhibit the weird, expressionless state they called *hwil*, Oria had more evident calm and emotional reserve than she seemed to realize. Certainly far more than the most controlled Destrye woman exhibited.

Oria had developed that reserve and used it like a shield that she retreated behind when she was displeased with him. He didn't know much about marriage—or women, really, since his relationship with Natly had been of an entirely different flavor—but he and Oria seemed to be growing farther apart rather than coming to know each other better. He'd thought if he could find ways for them to have sex, that the emotional and physical intimacy would bring them closer together. Instead, he seemed to be losing connection to her. As if with each layer of reserve he peeled away, she compensated by withdrawing behind other walls.

Like now. No time or opportunity to really deal with it, much as he'd like to broach the topic, because he hadn't exaggerated the dangers the approach of nightfall brought. He hadn't wanted to frighten her, but packs of wolves did prowl the mountains and his mother's hermitage still lay a distance off. Quite a distance, judging by the landmarks. Farther than he'd recalled. It had been so long since he'd made this journey, with so much happening in the interim.

Hopefully he hadn't badly miscalculated and put them in danger.

As if evoked by his thoughts, a wolf's eerie, hair-raising howl echoed through the dimming twilight. Buttercup danced restively, too well-trained to spook, but not complacent either. The warhorse had been raised in this area and knew that sound. Keeping his seat solid, his hands soft on the reins, Lonen flexed his calves in a signal to Buttercup. Were it only the two of them, this could be handled. Not easily, but he and Buttercup knew this sort of fight. Having Oria there changed everything.

The howl rang out again, joined by several more. Drawing closer. Wonderful.

"The wolves are that dangerous?" Oria asked softly, as if the creatures could overhear.

"I've fought them before. Nothing I can't handle," he assured her.

"I can feel your tension and anxiety, Lonen. Don't lie to me." She said it in that quiet tone, but the accusation stung. Nothing like having a wife who could read your mind.

"I didn't mean to lie, only to reassure you." The howls came from the side and—Arill curse them—from ahead. The wily creatures were outflanking them.

"If we're going to be a team, as you're always poking at me about, then you have to trust me to handle the truth," she replied, still sounding distant.

She had a point there. Perhaps that lay at the root of the barrier between them. They'd been coming closer to mutual trust, but then they found the mask and... With a mental wince he accepted that he might be the one creating that distance. "I'm not as civilized as I'd like sometimes," he admitted, squeezing an arm around her waist before reaching for his battle-axe. "Part of me is still the barbarian who'd like to wrap you up and keep you safe."

She glanced over her shoulder, her expression taking life with a soft—even affectionate—smile. "Will you throw me over your shoulder and outrun the wolves?"

"Tempting." The howls drew nearer, ringing them. "Though Buttercup can run faster than I can, and the wolves have us surrounded."

"Then we fight," she replied, as if suggesting a cup of tea.

"Or you could stay on Buttercup and escape while I hold them off," he countered, though without much hope.

"Oh no you don't." She twisted more fully, eyes flashing in the low light. "The last time you pulled that you ended up gutted by golems. You have me and you have Chuffta. Consider this practice for the duel."

It would be nice to practice as a fighting team without having their lives on the line, he thought sourly to himself, but he only nodded. "What does Chuffta say?"

The white form of the flying lizard winged through the deeply shadowed forest off to their left. "He sees ten wolves—three ahead, two behind, three to the left, two to the right. Ah, another ahead, so eleven."

Handy, he had to admit. "Can you feel the wolves' minds?"

She paused, disconcerted. "I can try."

He smiled to himself, pleased to have pointed out something she hadn't thought of. After a moment, she shook her head. "I can sense them, but remotely. To get a feel for the mind inside, I think I'd have to touch them, at least the first time getting to know them."

"That won't happen." Not while he had breath in his body. With a flex of his thighs, he halted Buttercup at a decent clearing—just wide enough for the horse to be able to maneuver, but ringed with dense trees that should funnel the approach of the wolves into a few directions. "What about defensive magic?"

"I suppose this is a good time to try." She sounded not entirely certain.

"Sometimes pressure brings out the best in us."

"I don't know what I'm doing, Lonen. I have no skill with grien magic."

"Blunt weapons work, too. Do what you can. Otherwise, don't worry about it."

Surprisingly she laughed. "Chuffta is eager to assist with fire. He's all excited."

"Tell him to burn away. I'll fight them best from the saddle. I'm used to avoiding Buttercup's head and neck. Be a burr and lie low against his neck."

"I could dismount."

The image of her on the ground, savaged by wolves, nearly stopped his heart. "No. You stay on, no matter what happens. Last resort, we run for it."

A howl pierced the forest twilight gloom, sounding like it was at his elbow. "Down!" he ordered. Buttercup, in full battle mode, spun at the flex of his knee and he swung his axe in an arc aided by the stallion's momentum—rewarded by the bite of iron into flesh and the pained yip of the wolf.

It dashed back. Just the scout, testing if they'd be easy prey. Yellow eyeshine glowed from the shadows ringing them, and he sent mental thanks to Chuffta for the count—otherwise his fear and the tricks of light might've made him certain there were far more.

Buttercup turned a tight circle, guarding all flanks. Three wolves charged at once. The horse reared, striking with iron-shod hooves, catching one wolf on the jaw and sending it flying. The other two struck in a well-timed pincer. Lonen got one in a solid, killing blow, but the other managed to sink teeth into the stallion's hind leg, attempting to hamstring him. Buttercup whirled, shaking it, and Lonen swung, sadly missing.

Four more wolves darted in on the open side, one going for the other hamstring, while several circled out and around, preparing to pounce at best opportunity. Too clever by half, using their numbers to worry them to death.

Chuffta's flame split the darkness, the green fire blinding as he swooped over the wolves, setting them alight. The agonized shrieking of the wolves rose with the stench of burnt fur and flesh. Oria, always so sensitive to the suffering of others, moaned. He made himself ignore her, unable to afford any distraction. Buttercup threw down his head, shoulders bunching, and punched out a double-mule kick, sending a snarling wolf into a tree.

Lonen barely registered that it fell limp, though one remote part of his mind ticked off the tally. One dead. Three down. Seven to go.

He blurred into battle mode, he and Buttercup working seamlessly to spin, hack, strike, slice, bite. And Chuffta became part of the deadly dance, swooping in before and behind the sharp edges of axe and hooves, blinding the wolves with fire, driving them back.

Two dead. Four down. Five to go. Slowly but surely.

When a wolf caught the edge of Chuffta's wing, he knew it by Oria's scream.

She'd been so good, clinging to the warhorse's neck

through all the stallion's twists, bucks and rearing strikes, as if she'd been born to riding. But now she sat up, lunging for her Familiar, overbalancing them.

"No!" Lonen thundered, dropping the reins to hold her in place. She thrashed in his arms like a wild thing as Chuffta went down, yanked to the ground by the snapping wolves, another pouncing to join the fray.

Oria shrieked wordlessly, but he held her with ruthless determination, urging Buttercup to attack. The stallion seized one wolf with his blunt teeth, immediately sinking his weight back. What the warhorse lacked in a piercing bite, he more than made up in sheer leverage. The wolf gave an agonized yelp, flying past them, abruptly silenced as Lonen ended it with a sweep of his axe.

Three dead. Four down. Four to go.

A wolf fastened on Buttercup's hind leg and the horse lurched. The one wolf still stood on Chuffta, snapping its jaws down as it dodged flame. Two wolves circled them, prowling closer, and another got up to join them, not dead yet, curse it.

Two dead. Three down. Five to go.

Lonen swung the axe back, trying to dislodge the wolf from Buttercup's leg. If it managed to hamstring the horse, they'd all go down with Chuffta. The stallion kicked, ineffectively. Oria still reached for Chuffta, screaming words in Báran now, such was her panic.

Too many targets. He couldn't fight every front. Chuffta might be lost, but he could still save at least Oria. Taking the risk, he wormed the hand holding her inside her clothes, the bare skin of her thigh above her stockings the most accessible. Steeling himself, he laid his bare hand on her skin and gripped hard.

Her scream froze his blood. Ruthlessly, he held on, resisting the reflex to let go. Until she sagged, weakened by the impact of his skin on hers. Thrusting the reins into her unresisting hands, he kicked an attacking wolf and swung down, killing it with a downward blow.

Four dead. Three down. Four to go.

Bashing it over the skull with the flat of the axe, he knocked the wolf off Buttercup's leg.

Four dead. Four down. Three to go.

"Go!" he shouted. Buttercup's haunches bunched as the horse leapt to obey. A wolf launched itself at Lonen's arm, fastening on with vising jaws. One on him, one on Chuffta. Where was the other?

Buttercup swung around. Oria's hood had fallen back, her hair sweeping in a banner of bright copper in the dying light.

"Run!" he howled.

"I. Will. Not."

And a strange hush ensued, as if time itself paused.

He could see it all. The wolf at his feet. Seven others on the ground. One on his arm. One on Chuffta.

One leaping for Oria.

Too far. Too late. Too slow.

Her magic filled the glen like a bore tide, crackling and crowding out the air. The trees seemed to bunch and shudder, drawing in as if inhaling. Then a storm blew out, a tornado of wind throwing him against a tree with stunning force. The wolf on him dislodged, taking a chunk of something with it. With a snarl, Lonen managed to bring his axe down, cutting its head off.

Five dead… He'd lost track of the rest.

Whirling, he lunged for Oria's last location—and found her crouched on the ground, Chuffta's limp form before her. Buttercup stood over her in guard position. Good steed. And the wolves… all limp carcasses. None moved.

Oria wept with heartbreaking sobs.

He forced himself to her side, his knees giving way, painfully smacking as they hit the hard-frozen ground. A distant part of him recognized with grim amusement that he could notice that minor pain when he felt nothing from his other, far more serious wounds.

"I can't hear him at all." Oria was sobbing so hard that he could barely make out the words. Her hands shook violently as they ran over Chuffta's limp and bloody form. "I've lost him. He's gone and I'm all alone."

It was the grief and fear talking, so he set aside the stab of injury at her careless words. "Oria, love." He rubbed a hand over her back, scanning the small clearing for movement, the black depths of the forest for eyeshine. "We have to move."

She turned on him, face contorted with tears. "Do you feel *nothing?*" she hissed, the words sharp as daggers.

"What I feel isn't relevant," he bit out, trying for calm. "We can't save Chuffta if we're all dead and if we stay here, we will be. Blood calls to predators and scavengers alike. We're hurt, weak, and vulnerable. Now gather up Chuffta and let's go."

"Why does it matter? He's dead."

He would've snapped back if she didn't sound so broken. For all Oria had been through, she'd still experienced so little of the hard blows the violent world dealt with abandon. It had been a long time since he wept over a fallen comrade. Later, he'd mourn Chuffta—but he'd learned to save the luxury of grief for safety. And not to declare death too hastily.

"Can you hear Chuffta when he's sleeping?" he asked, knowing the answer, but walking her through it with all the patience he could muster.

Oria blinked at him, eyes wide and owlish in her pale face, almost a hint of eyeshine in them, though human eyes didn't do that. His sorceress wasn't entirely human, however, so maybe…

"Well," she said slowly. "Usually there's *something*, but sometimes I don't."

"Gather him up, love," he urged gently. "Wrap him inside your cloak and keep him warm. He may yet survive."

She moved so hastily then that he might've laughed, had their circumstances been less dire. Climbing to his feet with a groan for how much he'd stiffened up even during the short stint on the cold ground, he hung his axe on the saddle and ran hands over Buttercup's haunch where the wolf had bitten. Blood—and the stallion stomped when he probed the tendon—but he seemed sound enough to ride. Good thing, as walking would see them finished off, no doubt.

Oria moved next to him, Chuffta in her arms under her shadowcat fur cloak. "Ready?" he asked. When she nodded, he lifted her onto Buttercup's back, grunting as his left arm nearly gave.

Oria caught herself, settled, and looked at him, her face pinched with concern. "You're hurt. I forgot."

"Nothing mortal," he assured her, swinging up behind her and sending the stallion into a fast clip up the trail in the same movement. Not a gallop or canter as the warhorse couldn't sustain that for the remaining distance, but a fast trot. "I'm more concerned about Buttercup. Anything you can tell me about how he's doing?"

She was quiet a moment. "He's hurt, too," she replied, sounding chagrined. "His hind leg pains him, and he's very angry. He's mostly picturing stomping on wolves."

"Can he make it?"

"He says he'll never let you down." She had an odd sound to her voice, kind of choked.

"Chuffta will be all right," he promised recklessly.

"It's not that." She swiped at her face. "I mean, it *is* that. I've never been through that, him crying for help in my head, and I felt his pain…" She trailed off. Took a deep, ragged breath. "I'm so angry with myself for letting *you* down. I utterly failed back there."

His heart squeezed, and he wrapped his good arm around her. "No, love. You did well."

"I panicked. I lost objectivity and just… lost control."

"You've never been in a fight like that before."

"How can you always forgive me?" She sounded almost exasperated, making him laugh.

"First, there's nothing to forgive. Second, I love you."

She sighed. "I'm not at all sure I deserve it, Lonen."

"That's the miraculous thing about love," he replied easily, pressing his lips to her hair. "It's there whether we deserve it or not." It felt good to say that to her, to remind himself of that truth. They could build trust over time, as long as the love remained.

She didn't reply and they rode a while in silence. She was sinking into a fugue of worry over Chuffta. He knew how that went, how the grief and despair could suck you under.

"What did you do?" he asked her, mostly to keep her talking. She'd used her grien magic in a different way—though still related to trees. Every bit of her grien magic that he could recall related to trees or plants, come to think of it.

"Do?" she sounded vague again, startled out of deep thought.

"Your magic—you did something to knock all the wolves down." And himself, too, though he didn't add that, as she'd only feel bad about it. The echo of those bruises throbbed through his spine.

"Oh." She shivered a little. "I'd kind of... forgotten."

A chill crept over him, too. Her magic hadn't been like this before, with the forgetting and losing herself. That foul mask played a part in it, no doubt.

"I was so afraid," Oria continued. "Chuffta was shrieking in my mind, calling me to help him, and I felt so helpless. And the wolf had you. I wanted them all to go away, just go away and leave us."

She sounded so afraid and tenuous, almost childlike, that he laughed, hoping the sound would hearten her. Smoothing a hand over her shining hair, he kissed it again. "You certainly accomplished that."

"What was it like?" she asked, after a long hesitation.

Surprised she didn't know, he chose his words carefully. It was tempting to gloss it, but that wouldn't help her learn the truth of her abilities. "Like time paused and all the trees inhaled, then blew out their breath all at once, in a fury."

She didn't reply to that, seeming to shrink inside herself.

"Oria?"

"That sounds so... unnatural."

Maybe he'd erred in describing it to her. "I recall at the battle of Bára that one of the sorcerers made tornados. Maybe that's how they start."

"That's right. I wonder if that's how it feels from the inside."

"Perhaps so."

Buttercup had begun to limp. The great-hearted horse couldn't carry them much longer. Had Lonen been alone, he would've walked. As it was, he might have to jog alongside, to keep up the speed. He could force himself to keep going that long, surely.

Just as he'd determined he'd have to, he caught sight of lights up ahead. Never had he thought he'd greet the sight of his mother's house with such a rush of sheer happiness.

"We're almost there," he said, to Oria, and to Buttercup, patting the horse's flank. "Only a bit farther, buddy, and you'll be in a nice warm stall with a pretty girl to tend your wounds."

Buttercup had his ears perked forward, picking up his already punishing pace with all the spring of a horse scenting food and rest.

"Your mother has girls as grooms?" Oria asked.

"My mother lives entirely with other women. Can you feel anything from Chuffta?"

"No, but he's still warm and flexible, so maybe he lives. I wish I knew more of how to tell. Even if he's alive, I don't know how to heal him." Her voice went ragged at the end.

"No worries there," he cuddled her close. "My mother will."

"Just who *is* your mother?" Oria wanted to know, sounding bewildered. They came around the bend in the path, and the hermitage stood before them, a single white candle alight in every one of the many windows. The double front doors opened wide, and rows of young women and girls spilled out, each carrying a lit candle, robes white as the snow that lay smooth and pristine all around the manse. A tall figure walked between them, her dark hair trailing on the snow behind her like a train.

"The question is," she called out in stern tones, "who are you, foreign sorceress?"

"Mother," Lonen called, wishing heartily that they'd arrived in better condition for this. "I'd like you to meet Oria. My wife, and Queen of the Destrye."

~ 5 ~

L ONEN'S MOTHER GAVE Oria a long, hard stare. "Odd," she commented with a blandness that didn't fool Oria for a moment, "I believed I retained the title of Queen of the Destrye."

Oria had never met Lonen's father, the late King Archimago—she'd only ever glimpsed him from the height of her tower—but the family resemblance to her son clearly shone in this woman's face. Tall, with broad cheekbones like Lonen, she possessed the same level gaze, granite in feel, though Oria couldn't make out the color from this distance. Her dark hair, like her son's, though glinting with silver threads, flowed thick and full down her back. If it hadn't been so long—and Oria hadn't imagined anyone could grow their hair to such an extreme—it would have rioted in curls as Lonen's did.

Lonen sighed. With him behind her, wrapped around her, she felt it, though he kept it inaudible.

"You were the first to teach me that people change and that crowns move from one person to the next," he called back, his words fraught with meaning beneath the surface. Buttercup had halted and they moved no closer, though she knew both man and horse trembled on the edge of fatigue.

There was some line in the snow-covered yard that Lonen observed—and waited for the invitation to cross. Chuffta lay limp as old lettuce in her arms. Not since she was a little girl had she not felt him in her mind at all. The loss left a hole in her, a shivering aloneness that ached with an almost physical pain. After her devastating loss of composure during the fight with the wolves, she hadn't wanted to belabor her grief aloud to Lonen, but her control frayed at the edges. She had no patience for pettiness at the moment.

"Is that why you've come at last, my prodigal son?" Lonen's mother asked, lightly mocking. "All this time you haven't bothered to visit. Now I perceive you're only here to inform me that I've been replaced."

"You accuse me of recklessness, still? I am a man grown, and king."

"How could I know?" she replied in that lofty voice. "You might as well be a stranger to me."

Oria felt Lonen set his teeth, the frustrated roil of his thoughts palpable. "Surely we could have this conversation in private, Mother," he answered. "In the warmth. I brought you a gift of a stardew. Or will you deny us your hospitality?"

She raised her brows, the dark wings of feigned astonishment clear in the candlelight. "You came equipped with a bribe? I can't decide if you've finally learned manners or if this is an example of improved political calculation."

Lonen growled deep in his chest, still unlikely to be audible to anyone but her. He also flinched emotionally, the barb hitting its target with the accuracy only close family could muster.

Oria had had enough.

"Your Highness," she called out. "I am indeed foreign and don't fully understand the ways of the Destrye, but where I come from, we don't leave anyone, let alone family, standing out in the cold, especially when they are exhausted, hungry, and injured. Snub me if you find it warranted, but your son comes to you with an open heart. You complain he hasn't visited. He's visiting now, and it seems you are intent on refusing the very thing you claim you've wanted."

The dowager queen's gaze landed on Oria again. The distance didn't allow for a good scan of the woman's emotions, but Oria might've detected a hint of surprise—and grudging respect?

"At least you didn't marry that ninny, Natly," she replied. "Come in then, and be welcome at my hearth."

Buttercup, as if understanding the words, immediately moved forward. "Nicely played," Lonen murmured in her ear.

"You could've warned me she'd be like this," she muttered back.

"I never know what she'll be like," he countered enigmatically, then halted Buttercup at the foot of the stairs leading up to the enormous house. Oria had never seen a structure so large made entirely of wood. Not even Arill's Temple. The manse seemed like it should fall over, but the edifice gave the impression of age and solidity.

One of the young women in the white robes handed her candle to her neighbor, curtseyed to Lonen, and held out a hand, keeping it a safe distance from Buttercup. "May I, Your Highness?"

"Please." Lonen swung down and handed her the reins, giving the subtle signal for Buttercup to regard her as a friend. Or so Oria assumed—mostly she heard Buttercup's suspicious alert relax, and the hurt and exhaustion creep over his mind. "He's injured," Lonen continued, taking a hold of Oria by the waist and lifting her down, then snagging his axe, "though not too badly, I think."

Another young woman stepped up, bringing her candle.

"I'll assist, Your Highness, and will bring in the packs."

"What happened?" The queen mother asked, waving the women on.

"We were attacked by black wolves not far from here."

"How many?" Her face sharpened with concern. Not as indifferent as she'd hoped to appear then. She turned and gestured them to accompany her inside. "And where?"

"Eleven. About an hour's fast ride."

Had it only been an hour? It had felt like forever. The cloistered warmth of the manse wrapped around them like a cloak, a vast fireplace in a large room clearly meant for receiving visitors emitted a blast of welcome heat. With a pang that felt far too much like mourning, Oria imagined Chuffta delightedly winging toward it.

"You fought off eleven wolves by yourself?" His mother sounded astonished. "Tell me—"

"I'd like to, and I will"—Lonen cut her off—"but we have a pressing problem for you."

"For me?"

"Show her, Oria." When she hesitated, he smoothed a hand over her hair. "You can trust her."

Oria highly doubted that, but she pushed the cloak back over her shoulders and presented Chuffta to the imperious woman. Devoid of his liveliness, the white scales not shimmering but dulled and spattered with blood, her Familiar looked much smaller than usual, limp in the cradle of her arms. She'd managed to fold his wings in before she gathered him up as Lonen had bade her, making sure the slender bones wouldn't pierce the soft, leathery skin, though she thought at least two were broken.

"Is that... a derkesthai?" In her hushed question, in her softening expression, wonder bloomed—and along with it a hint of a genuine woman under the cool exterior.

"Yes," Oria replied, relief along with the surprise. "He's my Familiar and a valued companion. Can you help him?"

"I can try, though I haven't seen a derkesthai in ages."

"I'm surprised you've seen one at all," Lonen commented.

His mother shot him an unamused smile. "Which only proves how little you know about me. Bring your Familiar in here."

She led them through the reception hall and through a doorway into a much smaller room, also furnished as a sort of parlor. With chairs, shelves of books, and another fireplace—though unlit at the moment—it looked to be a place for people to sit quietly. They moved right through it and into yet another room through a door on the opposite wall.

"No weapons in here," she directed, and Lonen didn't protest, leaving his battle-axe outside the door, leaning it against the wall blade-end down.

This room looked like it could be used for cooking, or perhaps some other craft that required clean surfaces. A large table sat in the center of the space, with no chairs, and taller than one useful for sitting. Lonen's mother nodded her head at it and went to gather tools from a far counter. "Lay him on there. I apologize that it's cool in this room."

As if summoned, another of the white-robed young women entered quietly and lit the fire already set in the fireplace at one end of the room. Just as unobtrusively, she left again.

Oria laid Chuffta, so fragile and nearly boneless, on the glazed surface of the table. The green of his eyes showed dully through his thin lids, more the color of the unripe olives from home, rather than the bright shine of new apples. She caught the sob rising in her throat, and Lonen put his hands on her shoulders, drawing her back against his strong body.

"Easy, love," he murmured. "My mother is the best there is."

His mother returned to them just then, flicking him a wry glance from eyes that were indeed the same shade of gray, and just as lushly lashed in black. They shone with incisive intelligence from a face far too imposing to be called pretty. She coiled up her hair with deft and practiced hands, pinning it with several sharp picks. The healers at Arill's Temple had used some sort of intuitive magic to assess wounds, but Vycayla turned to a tray of strange-looking instruments. She inserted something into her ears with long tubes that extended to a disk that she placed on Chuffta's little chest. Moving it around several times, intently listening, she made a hmming noise.

"Is he... dead?" Oria asked, needing to know, even as she dreaded the words. "Your Highness," she added hastily, hoping she hadn't further offended the woman in her anxiety.

"Call me Vycayla. And no, he's not dead, ..." She raised her brows at Lonen. "Did you bother to name this sorceress bride you captured?"

Oria didn't wait for Lonen to reply, riding on indignation and a rush of relief at the news. "My name is Oria, and I give you leave to address me by it. And I was not captured but married Lonen willingly, out of duty to my people and obligation to the Destrye. I don't believe I've given you cause to insult me by implying otherwise."

"Prickly. And arrogant. Perhaps unwise, as I'm treating your Familiar." Vycayla's gaze passed over her, reassessing, then flicked to Lonen. "I like her."

"I'm relieved," Lonen replied, even more drily. Oria began to understand his attitude about his mother.

"He seems to be in a deep sleep. Alive, but with a lowered

heart rate and respiration. Possibly a healing mode." Vycayla spoke in a dispassionate tone, her hands moving with professional expertise over Chuffta's body. She lifted her gaze to Oria's. "Is this something characteristic of derkesthai?"

"I don't know. He's never been injured before," Oria replied, feeling stiff in her embarrassment and ignorance.

Vycayla made a noncommittal sound, exactly like Lonen's. "Some internal damage, though light. The worst is these broken wing bones. I can set them so they'll heal cleanly, then treat him to accelerate the overall convalescence. For now I'll give him a bit of strength and let him rest, so he'll be in a better state for me to work on him."

"Thank you," Oria said with quiet fervor. "What is your price?"

Vycayla raised an amused brow. "Are you truly a sorceress?"

Lonen squeezed Oria's shoulders in some kind of warning, but she didn't see any reason to prevaricate. "Yes." She also wouldn't qualify it. Whatever she'd done in the forest, she could do again. And she'd pay any price to save Chuffta. She'd give herself over to the mask—even if she had to fight Lonen.

"Then I'll think of something appropriate you can do for me." A misty gray light glowed around Vycayla's hands, and Chuffta seemed to absorb it, his color moving closer to his usual iridescence.

When Baeltya, the junior healer back at Arill City, had treated Lonen, Oria hadn't been able to detect the flow of magic. She still sensed nothing magical, but seeing that light was new. "Are you an acolyte of Arill?" she asked, beyond curious. Behind her, Lonen choked a little, swallowing it down and squeezing her shoulders again.

Vycayla, hands still on Chuffta, gave her an arch look

without lifting her head, the flash of silvery gray through her lashes almost predatory. "The Queen of the Destrye is the head of Arill's Temple. You don't know much, do you?"

"About Dru and the Destrye, no," Oria replied evenly. "Though I dare say I know more about your people than you do about mine."

"You dare a great deal, indeed," Vycayla said, straightening and rubbing her hands together, her penetrating gaze studying Oria.

"Mother, the customs of Oria's people—" Lonen started to say, but Vycayla cut him off, sharp eyes never leaving Oria's face.

"Don't let your husband speak for you," she advised. "If you're to be Queen of the Destrye, you must speak for yourself. And stand on your own feet."

Oria shrugged off Lonen's restraining grip. Loath though she might be to do what his mother commanded, she also didn't need to be seen as weak. It was a valid point. "Surely there's a difference between enjoying the support of the man who loves me and leaning on him."

"Is there?" Vycayla shook her head slightly. "I don't agree." Despite her sharp tone, she picked up Chuffta with infinite gentleness and carried him to a basket before the fire. "There, sir. This will warm you. All right," she continued briskly as she returned, "strip off your shirt, son of mine, so I may see to your injuries."

"Yes, Mother," he answered, his voice as wry as the look he gave Oria. Another she couldn't quite interpret. He untied his cloak, fumbling a bit as his left arm hitched. Oria moved to help him, and he gave her a soft smile. She laid the cloak over a chair, then helped him pull the leather shirt over his head. Vycayla watched, not moving to assist, though Lonen had to bend over considerably for Oria to get the thing off. It was a frustrating exercise, but they managed. Oria smoothed her hair out of her face and took a look at Lonen, her mouth falling open at the sight of his ravaged arm.

"Lonen," she gasped in dismay.

"Better my arm than my throat—or yours, love." He gave her an affectionate smile and hitched himself onto the table, where his mother, apparently unmoved, brought a basin of warmed water and began washing the wound.

"Be still," she told him, though he hadn't so much as flinched, then patted him on the cheek, showing the first glimmer of maternal affection. "And be quiet. I have questions for your wife."

When she turned away briefly to rinse the bloody cloth in the basin, Lonen rolled his eyes at Oria and grinned in encouragement. He'd paled, however, the glassiness of pain and blood loss in his eyes. Oria still held his leather shirt and the softer one he'd worn beneath, heavy with the blood it had soaked up. She put them both aside, feeling a little woozy. Better sit before she fell over. Taking a chair by the fire, she sat where she could keep an eye on both her Familiar and her husband. "Questions?" she prompted.

"Who are your people, exactly?"

"I come from Bára. I'm the only daughter and third child of Queen Rhianna and the late King Tavlor."

"So you are the enemy," Vycayla noted, her attention on Lonen's wound.

"Bára and Dru have been enemies, yes," Oria replied evenly, though the subject wearied her. "I never fought, personally. When the Destrye armies attacked Bára, my father was killed, along with my two elder brothers. As the next in line for the throne, I negotiated a peace with Dru."

"Then why aren't you Queen of Bára?"

Oria bit back a sigh, watching Chuffta for any signs of waking. She dearly missed his sardonic commentary. "It's a long and complicated tale, but suffice to say my style of sorcery was not approved by our city elders and I was exiled. As I'd already married Lonen as part of our peace treaty, I traveled with him to Dru."

"Who's on the throne in Bára then?"

"My brother Yar."

"I gather from your tone that you don't approve."

Oria had thought she'd spoken quite neutrally, but no sense mincing words. "I don't. He's self-centered and emotionally unstable, especially since he contaminated his magic by summoning the Trom—the creatures riding the dragons that ravaged Dru last autumn. Even if he hadn't vowed to destroy Dru entirely, he wouldn't be a good king for Bára."

Vycayla threaded a needle and began stitching Lonen's wounds. He stared steadfastly at the wall before him, showing no reaction, though surely it hurt.

"You married Lonen before you came to Dru?"

"Yes, in the temple at Bára, according to the ways of my people." Oria waited for it.

Vycayla straightened, staring her son in the eye. "You haven't married this girl in Arill's Temple?"

Lonen gazed back. "Am I allowed to speak?"

His mother narrowed her eyes. "Don't be cheeky with me. You may be King of the Destrye, but I changed your diapers."

"Or handed me to a servant to do it," he replied gravely, then burst out laughing at the look on her face. "All right, all right. No, we haven't married under Arill's hand because we need a sponsor. Nolan has challenged me for the throne, and Arnon is his second. For Oria to serve as my second and then to be queen, we need to marry under Arill also."

"So *that* is why you've visited me at last."

"Yes."

"Self-serving to the end."

"I didn't think I'd be welcome without a compelling reason."

"You wouldn't have been," she snapped back.

Lonen only gazed back calmly. With the two of them nearly nose to nose, they were so obviously alike in almost every way. Except that Vycayla seemed to entirely lack Lonen's sense of humor or sunny outlook.

"On what grounds does Nolan challenge you?" she asked, going back to work with her needle.

Lonen grimaced—though for the pain or the forthcoming duel, Oria wasn't sure. "He believes I'm an inadequate king, that I allowed the Destrye to starve, and that I've failed to defend Dru." He left out the accusations that Lonen had been enchanted by Oria and wasn't in his right mind. Probably wise.

Vycayla snorted, a most unladylike sound at odds with her severe appearance. Perhaps she did possess some of the same humor. "What would Nolan have had you do—throw yourself bodily over the crops and aqueducts so the Trom dragons couldn't burn them?"

For a hermit far removed from the politics of Dru, Vycayla seemed to know a great deal about them. "He also disapproves of Oria and opposes having her as queen," he added carefully.

Vycayla glanced at her, but returned her attention to Lonen. "He'd send Oria back to the people that exiled her?"

"He suggested that I keep Oria as a concubine, spoils of war as the old traditions dictate, and take Natly as wife instead." Lonen spoke easily enough, but watched his mother closely. None of this conversation had been accidental then.

He'd been carefully managing how his mother heard the tale.

Vycayla paused as she processed that, then she glared at Lonen. "Your brother said this."

"In front of witnesses."

"And Arnon supports him."

"Arnon had little choice unless he wanted to openly defy his elder brother."

"Hmm." Vycayla continued stitching with meticulous patience, but her posture revealed her anger. "Would Nolan drag the Destrye back to being barbarians in every way?"

Lonen smiled, glancing at Oria, satisfaction in his gaze.

"What is Nolan's plan to fight the Trom and the dragons when they return, especially if our Báran sorceress is unhappily enslaved rather than being Queen of Dru as you promised her?"

"Nolan doesn't believe they will return."

Vycayla stopped, utterly astonished. "Did that fall rattle his brains? Perhaps I should be treating him."

Lonen laughed. "You know Nolan was ever one for seeing only what's in front of him. He can deal with trees well enough, but he will never believe there's a forest unless you can show him where it begins and ends."

"Hmm," Vycayla grunted noncommittally again, slathering some salve on the wound. "I thought he might gain wisdom over time, but apparently not. Whereas as *you*, my careless, feckless boy, have grown into quite a bit more of a measured man than I ever anticipated."

"Why, thank you, Mother. I love you, too."

She glared at him, but this time Oria saw the love in it. "So, that's your plan? Drag me back to Arill City—where you know I never intended to return—so you can marry Oria, win the duel, and secure the throne. Then what?"

"We haven't made exact plans," he temporized. "We've had many things to deal with," he added defensively when Vycayla raised one eyebrow at him.

"Left yourself open to Nolan there, my boy," she said. "Unwise."

"Lonen couldn't make a definite plan until we knew if I could wield magic outside of Bára," Oria inserted, pushing to her feet. "Now we know I can." She threw Lonen a defiant look when he scowled. She *would* use the mask, to save them all.

"You're quite the tiger," Vycayla commented, "defending this warrior brute of a son from his little old mother."

Oria gasped out an incredulous laugh before she could restrain herself.

Fortunately, Vycayla's eyes glittered with appreciation. "You need a plan," she said to them both.

Lonen opened his mouth, but Oria stepped forward. "Once Lonen is secure on the throne of Dru, we'll set the strategy to retake Bára in the spring."

~ 6 ~

B EFORE THAT MOMENT, Lonen would've sworn that his
wife and his mother were nothing alike. Now he gaped at
Oria, slim and pale, her hair shining in the firelight and spilling
in rivers of molten copper over the shadowcat fur. Large in her
exotically beautiful and piquant face, her eyes shone with
determination as she voiced this plan they'd never discussed.

"Retake Bára," he echoed, striving not to make it sound
like a question.

She returned his stare evenly, tension in the delicate line of
her jaw. "It's the only solution that makes sense. We have to
remove the threat at the source. Otherwise we'll be forever
defending Dru from Bára—and the Destrye will be absorbing
all of the losses. We have to take the battle back to them.
Strike them before they attack us, as your father did before
you."

His mother grimaced. "The old fool."

Oria looked shocked, but his mother didn't fool him. "He
missed you every day, too."

"Yes, well, I never said he didn't have excellent taste." She
blinked back moisture and looked him over. "Just the arm, or
anything on your lower half?"

"Just the arm," he confirmed. "I was lucky."

"You always were the best of fighters."

He had only a moment to savor the rare praise before she thumped the tip of her index finger smartly on the still tender scar over his eye. "This is new."

"But healing," he countered.

"Hmm." She made that sound he remembered well, making it clear she disagreed but wouldn't bother to argue about it. "What about this?" She probed his side, painfully digging her fingers into the sensitive new tissues there. "Something took a bite out of you."

Manfully, he held back all but a grunt of pain. "Golems," he ground out. "It's better than it was."

"I'd hate to have seen you when it was worse then," his mother quipped shortly. "Infection. And someone botched the healing of it. What in Arill were you thinking?"

"He nearly died," Oria volunteered. "He hid the infection from me until we reached Dru."

"Idiotic oaf like your father. I can't imagine how you thought you could win a duel against Nolan in this state. You'll be easy pickings for your brother unless we fix you up. I assume you're counting on returning for the duel before he can have you declared dead—how many days of the seven do you have left?"

His mother had always seen the bones of a problem quickly and concisely. "Five. Plenty of time."

"Hmm. Lie down. I'm going to do something about this. How's the derkesthai?"

Oria knelt, stroking Chuffta, lines of worry bending her mouth down. "He seems to be sleeping, as you said. Not so... dead-seeming."

"Excellent. I'll set his bones after I'm done with my son. You can go. Get cleaned up and eat. Go to bed if you like. I'll take care of these two."

Oria hesitated, her eyes owlish as they went to him in uncertainty at the abrupt dismissal. One of his mother's women slipped into the room, having been listening in case she was needed. "Come with me, milady," the woman said, curtseying.

"Go on, love," he said. "I'll be up soon. She doesn't eat meat," he remembered to add. "She needs grains, any vegetables you might have. Butter and cheese."

"Yes, Your Highness." The woman urged Oria out, and she went, his sorceress looking more than a little forlorn.

He'd have gone with her, at least to see her safely situated, but his mother's healing magic had already sapped his will to move. She'd grown stronger in the last years, and her power suffused him with Arill's green bounty—and his mother's sharp edges. A particularly strong surge made his innards cramp and he gritted his teeth against the gasp of pain.

"Yes, I know it hurts," his mother said, without the least bit of sympathy. She'd ever been that way. Even when he was a boy and ran to her with his skinned knees and the other small wounds of childhood, she'd never been the sort of mother to offer kisses or cuddle him on her lap. After a brisk lecture, she'd treat him—or oversee one of the junior healers—and send him on his way with a lecture on carelessness and orders to do better. "I'm going faster than usual," she explained, "or you won't make the seven-day deadline."

"I appreciate your help," he wheezed.

"Hmm. So, tell me how you ended up marrying a princess from Bára, of all places. A difficult little thing, for all she's pretty, in that exotic way."

"You don't like her," he said, not a question so much as laying it out there so they could get it over with. None of his family seemed able to see in Oria what he did. He'd grown resigned to it, but it still wearied him to have the same conversation over and over.

"Actually I do," his mother replied. "I said so, didn't I? She reminds me of me, in my youth." She glanced up with a wicked grin. "I never expected that you'd choose a wife so like your beloved mother."

"Oria is nothing like you," he said between his teeth. "She wouldn't abandon her family to go live in a remote place."

"No? I must point out, my foolish son, that's exactly what she's done. She left her Báran family to live with you in Dru."

He lay there, gritting through the waves of pain, contemplating that startling perspective. "It's not the same," he said, unable to muster a better argument.

"Hmm. How did you overcome her sensitivity to touch?" his mother inquired. She must've seen the answer in his face, because she chuckled. "Too rich. My son not only chooses a foreign princess, a magic-worker, but she's also a woman he can't bed. I'd love to hear the logic behind this thinking, since clearly you weren't thinking with your cock."

"Mother!"

"Oh, don't sound so shocked. I bore four children—I know how it works. Tell me why you made this astonishing choice."

"It wasn't exactly a choice at first," he admitted. "Father and Ion were dead, Nolan among the missing. I'd taken up Father's sword and crown. We lost so much going after Bára and I knew we couldn't withstand more conflict. When Oria proposed a marriage of alliance, I took it as the best solution among a bad lot."

"So you nobly sacrificed your future happiness and heirs to marry a woman you didn't love and could never touch?" His mother mocked him, but lightly. Distracted, perhaps, by the healing. She caught his eye, her gaze sharp, belying that theory.

"I love her," he confirmed. "I think I loved her the moment I laid eyes on her."

"Foolishly romantic, for you," she noted. "I'd never have predicted it."

"I know." He stared at the ceiling, remembering that moment, how he'd glimpsed Oria in that window, the magical winged lizard on her shoulder. "The war had gone on so long. We'd lost so many, been baking in that desert with no word from home. It's hard to explain, but even with Father and my brothers there, I'd never felt so alone. Hadn't known I could feel so utterly empty. When I saw Oria—it was like she'd stepped out of the paintings, like the one at Odymesen's chapel."

"Oria could be the twin of Odymesen's wife."

"Yes. And she's as powerful as those stories, or more." The sharper pains began to ease, the worst of the cramps backing off into dull aches. He struggled against the sweet exhaustion swamping him. "She can save us, Mother. If anyone can, it's Oria."

"Hmm. And after she's won the war for you? You can't live your entire life being faithful to a woman you can't bed or grow heirs on."

"We'll find a way. She's already overcome so many other problems. We'll find a way through that wall, too."

"Now there is the son I recall. Ever the optimist. I'm surprised the long campaign didn't kill that, too."

"I think it's all that allowed me to survive with heart and mind intact. Nolan—" He tried to think of the right words. "He's not the same."

"I'm sorry to hear that," she said quietly. "When he loses the duel, I'll persuade him to come back here with me. Perhaps

I can help."

He laughed, which became a cough—and something inside him loosened. An exquisite relief. "You're so sure I'll win."

His mother lifted her hands, then laid them on his cheeks, kissing him on the forehead as she hadn't done since he was a little boy, then gave him a long look—all Queen Vycayla. "You've grown into a good man, Lonen. You'll be a good king. And Oria will make a good queen. You two will bring together what was sundered. You'll win because you must." She patted his cheek with a bit of sting. "But stop protecting her so much. She's no fragile thing, and she won't grow the way she needs to with you shielding her. Sit up now—how's that?"

He pushed up, his abdominal muscles responding easily for the first time in what felt like forever, a sheer blessed relief. "You are a miracle worker."

"I know," she replied in a dry tone. "It's good you came. You had a great deal of scar tissue in there. When we return to Arill City, I'm going to have a conversation with Head Healer Talya. I'm not pleased with her work."

Somewhat sheepishly, he admitted, "I wouldn't let her work on me."

"Oh?" His mother raised that eyebrow, a world of questions in the gesture.

"She was ... unkind to Oria. I was unconscious and they put Oria in the charity ward, where she nearly starved and froze, though I'd told them she was my wife. Talya tried to keep her from me."

"Ah, politics. I don't miss that poisonous shit at all. Only for you—and Dru—would I return to that snake pit."

"I'm sorry to ask it of you."

"We all make sacrifices. This will give me an opportunity to clean house. Now, go to your wife, eat, sleep. I'll see you in the morning."

He went to put on his shirts again, but found them hopelessly bloodstained, wet and heavy with it. No wonder Oria had looked so dismayed.

"Leave them," his mother said. "I'll have something sent to your room." She went to the fireplace and gathered up Chuffta, blanket and all.

"How is Chuffta, really?" he asked. The derkesthai did look better, but remained limp and broken-looking. When his mother raised a questioning eyebrow, he added, "Is there anything you withheld in front of Oria?"

"I don't protect anyone's feelings," she replied firmly. "You should know that."

"True," he answered wryly.

"I'll take care of Oria's Familiar," his mother said with more gentleness. "Your sorceress will need him if you're to do what you hope."

"What do you—"

"Go away, boy. Do as your mother says."

He bent and kissed her cheek, the scent of her like home. "Yes, Mother."

She snorted. "Music to my ears."

THE SAME YOUNG woman who'd escorted Oria met him in the patient waiting salon, rising to her feet when he emerged, seeming not at all perturbed by his shirtless state. Probably she saw people in need of healing in all states of undress. He still had his cloak, so he slung that over his shoulders rather than carry it.

His mother preferred silence, and her ladies all observed that restful quiet, so he and his escort climbed the vast stairways and moved through the candlelit hallways without conversation. Nobody was about, most of the ladies no doubt taking to their beds early given the long, cold winter nights.

She paused outside a set of doors in the guest wing, curt-seying and gesturing him to enter. "Your things have been brought in," she murmured in dulcet tones that wouldn't carry, "You'll find food, wine, hot water for a bath, but ring if you need anything else, Your Highness, no matter the hour. Someone will be listening for you."

Lonen thanked her and went in. He didn't think he'd been in this set of rooms before, though most of the guest wing suites were much the same. No sign of Oria. A fire blazed in a fireplace tiled with a mosaic of lapis blues. Woven carpets and fur rugs covered most of the floors of gleaming wood, and a grouping of plush chairs and sofas clustered around the fireplace. On the other side of the sitting area, a carved wooden table set with two places held platters of food and jugs of wine and water. All apparently untouched.

"Oria?" He called out, crossing to the next room, which was a bathing chamber, tiled in more glossy blues, a large tub waiting and buckets of water steaming over another fire. Empty. "Oria!"

The bedroom held a large bed, draped in blue velvet co-vers and more soft furs. Tapestries of Lake Scandamalion in summer, under scorching blue skies and mountain peaks devoid of snow, covered the windows, hiding the snowy landscape with memories of warm weather.

Oria, still in her shadowcat cloak, sat in the middle of the bed, a small, still figure. With her head bowed, her hair fell shimmering around her like a second cloak. She might've been another tapestried illustration for all the life she evinced.

"Oria?" He took another step into the room.

And saw the gold mask gleaming dully on the coverlet before her.

Terror stabbed at him. Was she dead? Before he knew he'd moved, he snatched the cursed thing away from her. He'd forgotten it would be sent up with the contents of their saddlebags—a stupid, foolish oversight, one he hoped he wouldn't pay for. Or that she would.

But the mask had no blood on it, so he hid it in a fold of his cloak. Uncertain how to reach her, he called her name again. "Oria."

With the object of her mesmerized attention gone, Oria slowly came back to herself, like a statue of a woman coming to life. Movement returned in small ways, a hint of color flushing her pale cheeks. She lifted her head and stared at him, at first unseeing, then awareness returning. Her eyes, which had been mostly black, showed copper again as her dilated pupils shrank back to normal.

"Lonen." She blinked, long and slow, her lashes like coppery lace on her white cheeks. Then she smiled. Her smiles always transformed her, taking her from that intimidating otherness to lovely woman. Worry returned with awareness, too, her smile fading again as her eyes filled with it. "How is Chuffta?"

He shouldn't mind, that she asked after her Familiar first, since he himself was obviously fine. Still it stung a bit. "Mother is setting the bones now, but she believes he'll be fine by morning." Stretching the truth some, but better for her not to worry.

"Truly?" She searched his face for the lie. "Don't protect

my feelings."

Like his mother, indeed. "Time will tell, but I asked my mother again after she treated me and she says she's not painting a prettier picture than there is."

"You look so much better." She crawled across the bed, a bit stiffly, bearing witness to how long she'd sat without moving, and slid down from the raised height. Her feet made no sound on the thick rug as she came around the bed to him. She still wore her fur-lined stockings—she'd at least had the presence of mind to remove her boots—and still wore her gloves. At least she hadn't touched the mask with her bare hands. He'd like to think she'd made that choice out of caution, or being mindful of her promises to him, rather than absent-mindedness.

Running those gloved fingers over his bare abdomen, she marveled. "You've actually regained muscle. This is incredible."

"My mother has considerable skill."

"So I see. I have many questions for you." She followed the caresses of her hands with her gaze, then looked up at him through her lashes, coppery eyes lively with golden flecks, her smile a sensual smolder. "You look even more like a barbarian like this, wearing only your fur cloak."

Helpless to resist her allure, he fought the flood of heat, his cock engorging. She hummed a little, no doubt sensing it in him, and slid her hands over his flat belly to the ridge in his pants. Tossing the mask onto the bed, he caught her wrists barely in time before she seized him and made him forget everything.

She tracked the movement, gaze going to the mask, then to his face, her expression both chagrined and defiant. Had she forgotten it was there? Hoped he hadn't seen her with it somehow? Or, most likely, this sudden seductive move had been an attempt to divert his attention. "What happened to your promise not to touch the mask without me present?" he asked.

"I didn't touch it," she replied with heat. "I only studied it."

"You and I both know you can commune with it without actually touching it. You're splitting hairs to cover that you're in the wrong."

Her face flooded with angry color. "You can't keep it from me, Lonen."

"I can." He kept ahold of her wrists, even when she tugged at them. "Especially if you won't keep your word."

She shrugged in his grip, nonchalant, as if breaking her word didn't matter, as if his anger didn't bother her. "You have no right to decide—"

"I have every right," he snarled, beyond frustrated with her. "More, it's my duty. Even if I hadn't vowed as your husband to protect and nurture you, even if I weren't your king and charged to see to your well-being along with all of my realm, even then I'd keep it from you."

Ceasing her struggles, she gazed at him in consternation. "I'm going to need that mask, if you want me—"

"Don't you get it, Oria?" His rage fell apart, leaving ragged desperation behind. "I don't care about any of that as much as I love you. None of it is worth that price to me. Dru and the Destrye can go hang if it means sacrificing you. I can't bear to lose you."

"You'd sentence your land and people to destruction—and mine, too, most likely—for one person?" she demanded. "That makes no sense."

"I don't care." He dug in, aware he was being hopelessly stubborn, unwilling to change his position.

"Lonen…" She said his name in a broken whisper. "Don't *you* get it? That's exactly what Nolan accused you of. He thinks I enchanted you, enough that you'll abandon your duty to your people for me."

"Not because of magic," he countered. "Out of love."

"It's the same in the end."

"It's not. Love is something good and pure, not some perversion of magic. If you'd enchanted me, it would be a kind of control, and you don't do that."

"Arguably, if I had that kind of hold on you, you wouldn't know it," she countered, resuming her struggles. "Let go of me, you brute."

"No." He held her easily, that dark side of his nature relishing that he could. His sorceress. Powerful, lethal, magical—but his. He drew her closer against him so that the silk of her hair and the shadowcat fur slid along his skin, the fullness of her breasts and litheness of her body an enticement that scrambled his brain. She glared at him, fury unabated, mouth pursed in rebellion. "If I could kiss you, I would," he told her, his voice coming out rough. "I'd kiss you until you forgot everything but me."

Stilling, she leaned into him, her face reflecting the same hunger that plagued him. "Then do it. Kiss me and make me forget."

With a groan he leaned in, beyond tempted. Only the memory of the way she'd screamed when he touched her thigh restraining him from the reckless need to try. How much worse would it be on her tender mouth? Instead he brushed his lips over her hair, at last letting go of her wrists to enfold her in a desperate embrace, crushing her against him. The need to touch her, to be inside her, ground at him with a deep-seated craving.

"I wish I could," he said. "You have no idea how much."

"I have some idea. And I love you, too, more than I can find words to say." Her voice was muffled where her cheek lay against the fur of his cloak. "But I think even with kissing and touching we'd still fight."

He laughed, kissing her hair again. "Yes, but the making up would be sweeter."

She shifted, and her gloved hand glided between them, gripping his shaft as tightly as he'd held her wrists, eyes sparking with delight at her revenge. "This is sweet as it is," she noted. "Unless you're still sore?"

Surprised to note he felt no pain, he shook his head. His mother must've healed that too. He only hoped that came as a residual effect of the overall healing, rather than that she might've sensed the chafing from the repeated stimulation of Oria's velvet gloves the night before. An excellent lesson in how something apparently soft can be unbearably rough, given repeated exposure.

"Grasp the bed post," Oria told him, cool and arch.

"Excuse me?" Momentarily baffled, he glanced at the post beside him.

"You heard me—and you owe me, barbarian." She raised her brows in challenge. "Better, put your back to it and lace your hands behind."

Arousal spiked, and he did as she bade, having to shrug back his cloak to stretch behind him and link his hands together. The newly healed muscles in his arm, chest, and belly tingled. "What are you up to?"

"Whatever I want," she replied, eyeing him. "Does that hurt?"

"Not in the way you mean."

She pushed the cloak more fully off his shoulders, raising

herself on her toes to do it, then rounded her hands over his shoulders and chest. Then she reached up to remove the tie that kept his hair pulled out of his face. "You are a gorgeous man," she murmured. "Have I ever told you that?"

"No." And he found himself strangely warmed by her regard. "I'm a scarred and ugly brute, in fact."

She exhaled warm breath over his nipple. "You're so wrong." Her hands worked to unfasten his pants.

"Oria…"

"Be still. Or do I have to tie you there?" Her mouth curved in a sly and sexual smile, reminding him of the times he'd said as much to her.

He dragged in a breath as she tugged his pants down, and the air burnt in his lungs, ragged. The pants only went so far, stopping at the top of his boots and bunching there. He eyed the open doorway, hoping none of his mother's ladies would come to check on them. What an eyeful they'd get—him partly naked, fully erect, ruthlessly exposed, while Oria knelt down before him and formed her long, shining hair into a noose that…

"Holy Arill," he choked out.

~ 7 ~

THERE WAS A lovely power in seducing him this way. Holding his shaft firmly by the root, Oria fixed him in place as she teased him with the silken length of her hair. His eyes glazed over, his face going hard with arousal, those veins in his temples bulging. Her warrior, at her mercy.

He'd been correct that she'd started the seduction with the object of distracting him. No sense at all in them fighting over the mask as she'd resolved to learn how to use it. During the time waiting for him, realizing she was alone with the mask, she'd taken the opportunity to study it. Testing herself as she had with the freezing lake water, seeing if she could have it close and available without losing control of herself, and it.

She could use guile to coax Lonen along, much as he did with her. Two could play that game.

But, as it always did between them, the rush of passion took over, and she forgot that she'd intended anything but enjoying him. Lonen looked incredibly enticing this way, framed by fur and leather, his masculine strength leashed at her request. She began to understand why he liked it so well when he had her at his mercy, bound and crying out her need.

"This is my mouth on you," she murmured, giving him those words back, sliding her hair to tease and tighten. She added hot breath, and he moaned, leaping in her grip. She firmed it, then stroked, wishing she could use her mouth on him in truth, needing more ways to touch him.

Oil. He'd wanted oil.

"Stay like that," she ordered, rising to her feet. Tugging at his chest hair, sharply enough to get his attention, she delighted in the frustrated flex of his muscles. Perhaps all the physical power didn't belong to him. "If you move, I won't play anymore."

His gray eyes glinted with fierce determination. "I could convince you."

"No. I'm resolved." She allowed her long skirts to brush the head of his cock, savoring how his mouth tightened, the groan rising from him like a growl.

"Oria…" He dragged out her name on something very like a plea.

"Are you begging me?" she crooned, then laughed when he snarled. "I'll be right back."

He muttered something as she walked away, swaying her hips more than usual to add to his torment. On the supper table she found what she'd hoped for—a vial of oil pressed from olives. Setting it on the hearth to warm a bit, she stripped off her clothes, putting on his spare leather gloves instead of her velvet ones. They were too big, of course, and thicker than she'd like for this, lined to keep out the cold, but better than the velvet that had chafed him so viciously.

Retrieving the oil, she returned to him, wearing nothing but the large gloves, cloaked only in her hair. She thought she might look silly, but his gaze fired and his body flexed at the sight of her. Immensely gratifying. "Hold still," she purred, then drizzled the warmed oil over his chest.

He gasped, cursing through clenched teeth, and his magnificently muscled thighs tensed.

"Too hot?" she asked innocently.

"You'll find out how it feels when I get my hands on you," he promised, his voice rough.

"*If,*" she replied, with emphasis. "It depends on how good you are."

"Oh, Oria, love. I thought I'd repeatedly demonstrated that I'm *very* good, and—" He threw back his head, body arching and throat straining, as she allowed a drop of the warm oil to fall on the head of his cock. "Fuck!" he shouted.

"Turnabout is cruel, isn't it," she taunted. Pouring more oil into the palm of her glove, she set the vial aside and ran her hands over his chest, rubbing the oil in. He watched her through slitted eyes, the gray sparking silver with promises of retribution. She paused to toy with his nipples, as he did so often to hers, pinching them so he hissed. He strained toward her, not touching her bare skin, but clearly wanting to. Dragging her hands down his body, she knelt again, taking up the vial to pour more oil over his cock, enjoying the sight of the golden liquid coating his turgid member, and rolling off in beads. "We're getting oil on your mother's carpets," she noted, opening her eyes wide as she looked up at him, feigning concern.

"Ask me if I care," he growled.

She laughed—and it felt like ice melting. Even naked she was warm again. Chuffta would be all right. Lonen looked better than he had since before the golem battle. Cupping his heavy balls in one hand, watching his face for the right pressure, she worked his shaft with the other. He liked it hard and fast, she'd learned—a curious opposition to the meticulous patience he showed in tormenting her.

He jerked in her hand, hips thrusting as a groan rose out of him and he ground out a shout of pleasure, his seed spurting to land on her naked breasts. He watched in avid delight, so she kept milking him, rubbing his seed into her breasts, her own arousal so keen she nearly orgasmed then and there.

Lonen sagged a moment, breathing as hard as if he'd run a race. Then he lifted his head and gave her a menacingly silvery glare. "My turn," he said silkily. "Give me my gloves."

Sensual alarm thrilled through her and she started to rise as she pulled them off.

"No." He unlaced his hands, flexing them, then took the gloves and pulled them on. "Lie back, right there. Knees up. Thighs parted."

Trembling, she obeyed, very aware of displaying her slick arousal to him. He gave her a knowing smile. "Don't move," he cautioned her, and went to a cabinet near the bed. His grunt of satisfaction made her shiver again. What now?

He came around the bed, crawling on hands and knees, for all the world like a stalking predator. Naked now, hair hanging around his face in black snarls, he grinned as if he might devour her, holding something in one hand that she couldn't quite see.

"Pull your knees back, love, so I don't touch you."

"What is that?"

He stopped between her spread thighs and held it up, showing her. Carved of some smooth material, it looked like a wooden cock, polished and gleaming smooth. And awfully large. "Is that…"

"Yes," he hissed, his smile wicked. "It absolutely is." He sat back on his heels, lowering the thing and dragging it through her wet folds. She shook, moaning, and he nudged her entrance with the rounded tip. "This is my cock," he murmured, "and I'm going to fuck you with it."

Her moan took on a desperate edge as he pushed it into

her, filling and stretching.

"Hold wide apart," he coaxed, pushing it deeper, and now leaning over her, braced on one arm beside her head. "It might be easier for you on hands and knees, but I want to see your face—is that all right?"

The soft question from her predatory lover came as a surprise. She smiled at him. "I want to see your face, too."

"My beautiful sorceress." He pushed the phallus into her, working in and finding her depth. She arched her back at the pleasure, losing all breath. "There we go," he murmured, then began sliding it in and out of her, alternating several short strokes with one or two longer ones. On the deepest penetration, he'd stroke her pearl of pleasure with his thumb.

"Lonen," she panted, in a full frenzy, digging clawed fingers into the furry rug.

"Yes," he replied, staring into her eyes, black mane and molten silver. "Mine."

"Yes," she replied, and convulsed, letting the climax sunder her, imagining that it was him inside her.

And that nothing could ever come between them.

SHE LUXURIATED IN the hot bath as Lonen added another bucket of the heated water. "It's big enough for both of us," she pointed out.

"But not so big that I could avoid touching you," he answered, dipping a cloth in the water and using that to sponge clean himself.

Sometimes she thought he remembered the restrictions

better than she did. He'd so thoroughly invaded her intimate self that it was easy to forget he wasn't another part of herself. "Maybe it wouldn't be that bad..." she trailed off at the incensed look in his eye.

He pointed at her inner thigh, where she'd lifted a leg out of the water to soap herself. "And that?" he asked, in a dangerous tone.

She looked, surprised to find a handprint on the inside of her upper thigh, red and rough, as if she'd been scorched. "I forgot about that."

"I only hope it's not a permanent scar," he said, looking grim. "I'm so sorry."

"Don't be." She'd been wild with grief and panic, and his searing touch on her skin had jerked her out of it. "It doesn't hurt and you only did what you had to do to save us all."

"Hmm." He didn't say more, that wordless sound very like his mother's—and one that likely meant he didn't agree but wasn't planning to argue.

"What is this place?" she asked, to change the subject, sure, but also because she couldn't stand the curiosity any longer.

"Part healing center, part religious retreat, part refuge," Lonen said, sitting on a chair beside her, completely at ease with his nudity. His manhood hung lax and heavy between his partially parted thighs. If she could, she'd reach over and stroke him to arousal, just to see the transformation. As it was, his organ twitched, swelling slightly. "Are you listening?" he asked.

Her gaze flew to his face, her own heating with chagrin. "Yes. Sorry."

He spread his thighs wider, bracing his hands on them. "No apology needed. Look your fill—but I'll save the explanation for when you're paying attention."

"I'm paying attention," she replied primly, yanking her gaze away for good measure.

He chuckled, sounding darkly pleased. "Many a man would give a great deal for his wife to look at him the way you look at me. I like to look at you, too."

She didn't have to glance at him to verify that his gaze lingered on her breasts where they thrust above the water. They should both be sated, but desire coiled lazily in her stomach, demanding as ever. "You were telling me why your mother lives here," she reminded him.

"Well, that's a different tale, but I suppose they're inter-connected." He sat back in the chair, stretching out his legs to the fire, adjusting himself as he did—most fascinating. "A number of years ago, when the golem depredations had become so great that we began to fear that Dru and the Destrye would be destroyed, my mother and father had a truly epic argument."

"She lived with you then?"

"Yes, and served in the traditional role of High Priestess to Arill, along with being Queen of Dru."

This was something he'd never mentioned all those times that they'd discussed Oria's role in Dru. "I'm not a healer, Lonen. You know that," she felt compelled to mention.

He waved that off. "It's traditional, but not mandatory. Not every queen has been also a priestess of Arill's. It's not a concern."

Apparently part of being married to someone involved letting some battles go unfought. Lonen sunnily declared it wasn't a concern and she wouldn't solve the problem by arguing with him about it. Besides, she could deal with that once they scaled the several chasms between now and her being ratified as queen.

"Was the epic argument an unusual occurrence?" she asked instead. She began vigorously soaping her hair. The luxury of hot water to bathe in was something she'd once taken for granted—and never would again.

Lonen laughed, an affectionate shading in it. "Well, like all husbands and wives, they fought at times. And like all Destrye, they argued loudly and passionately."

Oria had never once heard her own parents argue beyond a mild disagreement. Theirs had been a temple-blessed marriage, a union of perfect harmony. But Oria had opened her eyes to all the assumptions she'd made in her youth, and in that moment she wondered if they'd been truly harmonious or simply creating the appearance of it. Could she herself pretend not to disagree with Lonen? She'd learned to fake the serene state of *hwil*, so she could certainly recreate her mother's demeanor of being sweetly loving and agreeable—along with the surface appearance of a lovingly harmonious relationship with Lonen where they never disagreed. But to what end, to playact for what audience?

"So, you don't mind that I fight with you?" she asked, squinting at him through the suds.

He paused, momentarily confused by the changed of topic, then grinned. "Oria, love—if you stopped arguing with me, I'd be worried you'd taken sick."

"Ha ha." She made a face at him and sunk under the water, rinsing her hair. When she surfaced, he'd scooted his chair closer, leaning his forearms along the tub's rim.

"Seriously," he said, gaze calm, face grave. "I value that you'll be a queen with the force of will to argue with me—as long as you respect that I won't cave to you, either."

She gazed back at him a moment, certain he referred to the mask that they both knew still lay on the bed, its magical hum an alluring background song that teased her senses, like the scent of rich gravy making her hungry for a meal she hadn't known she wanted. He leaned back again, breaking the tableau.

"So, yes—they fought at times, usually loudly, but this was different. By then our scouts had discovered that the golems that plagued us came from Bára, and my father wanted to take all the warriors of the Destrye and set out to make a last stand: destroy the makers of the monsters killing us inch by inch, or die doing it."

Oria soaped vigorously, wishing she could as easily scrub the guilt from her conscience. All those idyllic years of living in her tower in Bára, and she'd had no idea that her people had plagued their ancient barbarian enemy, rather than the other way around. "Your mother disagreed?"

He shrugged in his chair. "She thought we couldn't win. But that's not why they fought. Because the warriors and armies would be leaving Dru, the rest of the people couldn't fight off the golems on their own, so my father planned for them to leave. The women, children, the sick, infirm, elderly, scholarly—anyone *not* a fighter—would travel in a caravan to a land on the other side of these mountains. He wanted my mother to lead them."

She rinsed once more, then stood in the tub, taking the towel Lonen handed her and wrapping up in it. "Do you want to empty the tub?"

"No need." He scooped a bucketful of water out and emptied it down a drain hole, then added more hot water to the tub.

"There's plenty of hot water still," she pointed out.

"I know." He grimaced. "But it feels wasteful, even in this place of abundant water. Old habits."

"It's dirty."

"Your dirt is my dirt." He winked at her cheerfully and sank in with a happy sigh. He fit, but barely. They definitely couldn't have both been in it and not touched. He had a knack for assessing dimensions like that, which she utterly lacked.

"Queen Vycayla didn't want to lead the caravan?" she prompted.

"No. She wanted to come with us to Bára."

"And fight?" Oria couldn't contain her surprise.

"And fight," he confirmed. "Many of the Destrye women have learned to fight in recent years. With us so hard-pressed, it became a necessity, though the men still have a hard time with that. My mother pointed out it was ridiculous to plan to commit our entire fighting force, but confine the effort to the male portion of it. Failing that—as bringing women into battle was a tree far too tall to climb for our more traditional sorts— she wanted to stay in Arill City and defend it in the absence of the warriors."

"That makes sense. Why forsake all the defenses already in place?"

"My father… he had more than a bit of traditional barbarian in him." Lonen gave her a rueful smile as he soaped his hairy self in demonstration. "I come by it honestly. He couldn't abide the idea of the Destrye women in battle—and he was convinced that they'd fall to the golems in his absence if they remained in Arill City. He, and many of his advisors, felt that worrying about the women would be too distracting for the male warriors. My father finally issued an edict forbidding the queen—or anyone at all—from remaining in the city environs once he departed."

"Ah." She understood now—and could see herself making a similar choice. "So Queen Vycayla left in protest."

"Yes and many of the women went with her."

"They don't all look like fighters."

"Not all of them are. Some are healers, priestesses of Arill. Others have various skills and crafts. Some are lovers of other women or have their own reasons for eschewing the company of men. My mother meant to show the idiocy of my father's edict by removing herself from him and the palace, and ended up creating a new way of life."

"Ah. So that's why there was that… tool, you used on me."

He grinned at her, a wicked slant to it. "I found a similar one here before when we visited. I was younger then, and didn't figure out what it was right away. I was hoping I'd find one for us here. I have a number of ideas for ways to use it." His voice dropped into those sensual tones that always undid her.

She decided not to contemplate that too much, as she'd promised to pay attention. "Why did she come here, so deep in the mountains?"

"This used to be the summer palace, and it's one of the few places in Dru with plenty of water, though the winters are harsh. They planted crops for food, hunted, and offered healing services to anyone who traveled here, in exchange for other goods. That's what the white candles in the windows mean—an offer of safety and succor to travelers."

"And they succeeded."

"They did, and proved the point that they could survive without the men to protect them. Even before we left, it was clear my father regretted driving her to such an extreme with his ultimatum. We made the trip and visited a few times before we left on campaign, and they reconciled to an extent. But she refused to return to Arill City unless he allowed the women the choice of staying there or joining us on campaign, and he refused to consider it. Finally, when supplies were readied and we set out for Bára, and the caravan with all the others departed in the other direction, we left Arill City completely empty, as my father had decreed."

She mulled that over, and he took the pause as an opportunity to dunk his head and rinse his hair.

"But they could've come back when the army returned," she said when he surfaced, "like the people in the caravan did."

"Some of them did, sure." He stood, water sheeting off of his magnificent body, and she hastily handed him a towel instead of gawking. She'd meant it when she called him gorgeous. The scars only emphasized everything about him that appealed to her, and she relished the secret glee that she'd found her own barbarian, straight out of the pages of the old books. She'd never quite understood why his large and powerful body affected her so deeply, but some feelings went beyond rational explanation. And to have found a man of Lonen's loving nature with it...she'd been impossibly lucky. She couldn't imagine living without him.

"Do you think she couldn't bear to return, with King Archimago gone?" she asked, feeling her way around the question.

Lonen scrubbed the towel over his face and beard, then gave her a somber look. "I think they both bore a great deal of guilt over the separation, and that they'd both been too stubborn to reconcile. Under the best of circumstances, either would've been bowed by the grief of losing the other. Being estranged like that..."

Oria swallowed, surprised to find her throat tight with tears, her eyes prickling with unexpected grief.

"Here now," Lonen said, easily stepping over the high rim of the tub and coming to her. He wrapped the towel around her and embraced her over it, placing a gentle kiss on her wet hair. "What's wrong? Don't cry."

"Oh, I'm not." Impatiently she rubbed her nose and wiped the tears away. Then she looked up at him. "I don't want that to happen to us."

He gazed back at her, eyes misty gray with like feeling. Though only a moment elapsed, it felt eternal and fraught.

Then he cracked a grin. "Easily accomplished. If you ever try to move away from me, I'll simply find you, toss you over my shoulder, and carry you back."

She wrinkled her nose at him. "You think you could, you brute."

"I think you'd love it," he returned with a wicked sparkle. To prove his point, he lifted her and laid her over his shoulder—though the brutishness was mitigated by his care to make sure the towels stayed between them and their skin didn't touch—and he smacked her upraised, cloth-covered bottom, striding into the other room. "For now, I'm hungry for food. Even if there is no oil for my bread."

"We could ring for more," she pointed out, breathless from being upside down—and a bit from that sexual thrill. "We might need it for other things, too."

"I like the way you think, my love."

~ 8 ~

H E WOKE LATE—WELL into the morning, judging by the slant of the wintry sunlight streaming into the sitting room. The tapestries remained over the windows in the bedroom, shrouding it in shadow, but the doorway to the room beyond showed considerable daylight.

And no Oria.

Abruptly and fully awake, and with a curse, he leapt from the bed and to the locked cabinet where he'd stowed the mask. Still locked, but he retrieved the key from where he'd put it—hidden while Oria was tending to nature's call, and while he loudly thought of other things—and unlocked it. The mask gleamed with sullen light within. He even touched it, just in case it wasn't real, though Oria couldn't create illusions—not that he knew of, anyway—and found it unnaturally warm. Foul thing.

Breathing a sigh of relief, he locked the cabinet again, and considered swallowing the key. That would provide a few days of reprieve, theoretically, but as for that, Oria could simply have the cabinet chopped apart. Besides, the mask did belong to her, and she did need it. He couldn't destroy the thing, or her knowledge of its existence. They could only work with it.

Finding clothes laid out for him, he swiftly dressed, then pocketed the key. Telling Oria the sad tale of his parents' separation had been interesting—and had affected him deeply, too. He hadn't had much cause to think back to that epic argument, or the reasons for it, over the ensuing years. At the time he'd been headstrong, full of warrior pride and the arrogance of a young man in the prime of his strength. He'd been angry at his mother, laying all the guilt at her feet. She hadn't supported his father. She'd abandoned them all. Stubborn, unreasonable, callously independent, arrogant, cold-hearted. With a wince of deep chagrin he recalled all the faults he'd accused her of, both in his wounded son's heart, and aloud, griping with his brothers.

Never once had he thought about what his father had driven her to by issuing his ultimatum, so determined to have his way. *I don't want that to happen to us*, Oria had said, with that stricken look on her face. He'd made her laugh, distracting her, but for an endless moment the knowledge had throbbed between them that they very well could face an irreconcilable battle exactly like that.

And with far less history of connection between them to see them through it. If his own parents, after four children together and decades of marriage couldn't resolve their differences…

He would learn from this cautionary tale. That's all there was to it.

All vestiges of the dinner they'd shared had been cleared away, replaced by the cold remains of breakfast. He must've been sleeping like the dead if all that activity hadn't wakened him. He grabbed a muffin and wolfed it down, savoring the tang of dried fruit. It only added to the irony of it all, that his mother and her women ate so much better than the royal household in Arill City did.

Determined to find Oria, he stepped out the doors. A

young woman leaning against the wall smiled and curtseyed. "Good morning, Your Highness. May I escort you?"

"I'm looking for Her Highness the Queen," he replied, studying her. She seemed familiar.

"Certainly. Queen Vycayla is in her morning room. Allow me to—"

"I meant Her Highness Queen Oria."

The woman's smile turned wry as she gestured for him to accompany her. "Not 'Her Highness' and not 'queen,' yet, I think—or you wouldn't be here to take our lady away with you, Your Highness."

"I see gossip flies with its usual speed," he observed.

"Oh yes. The juicier, the faster it flies," she agreed cheerfully. "And the betting pool grows on what you'll decide, now that you are King of the Destrye."

Decide—about what? He gave the woman a longer look. "I know you... Alyx."

She grinned, and he saw past the white robe and older face to the young woman she'd been, in fighting leathers and training alongside them. The Destrye women had a difficult time going toe-to-toe with the bulkier men, particularly when upper body strength allowed them to wield heavier weapons. Some like Alyx, however, developed the speed, agility, and sheer tenacity to have beaten a number of men, to the male warriors' everlasting chagrin—and not a little resentment. When Queen Vycayla left, Alyx had gone with her.

"Good to see you, too, Lonen," she replied. "Though I never expected to call you my king."

"Believe me, no one was more surprised than I." He exchanged grimaces with her for all that had happened since their mutual youth. Then he realized what she'd meant, that the women fighters wondered if he'd change his father's decree on their status. "Do you?" he asked. "Call me your king."

She shrugged, staring down the hall. "That depends on whether you earn my fealty."

A sticky problem. By law his mother's hermitage and lands belonged to Dru and fell under his rule, but his father had been understandably unwilling to press the point. They'd drawn water from the lake, but hadn't required taxes or tithing. So much so that it hadn't occurred to him to access the stores here to alleviate the food shortage in Arill City. Changing the law regarding the women fighters would cause trouble in various quarters, particularly the traditional and stodgy ones, but that would be a small price to pay for additional food and healthy warriors for the defense of Dru.

Besides, Oria would be pleased. Anything he could do to balance her sacrifices and the inevitable friction for her of living in a foreign culture would be worth it. If she never wanted to leave him, he could neatly avoid the ramifications of dragging her back. That was just good strategy.

He stopped, and faced Alyx. "As far as I'm concerned, Dru needs every warrior we can get. I would be privileged for you and your sisters to fight alongside me."

Something fierce and bright shone in her face, and she went down on one knee, bowing her head. "My king, I offer you my fealty."

He laid a hand on her head, a strange set of emotions passing through him. How angry his father would be. How his older brother Ion would've mocked him for womanly softness and sympathy. So odd that he could miss them with such grief—and also take such perverse delight in defying their ghosts.

"I accept. Of course," he added lightly, drawing her to her feet, "I might lose the throne to Nolan and you'd likely be out of luck there." Definitely out of luck, as Nolan would be outraged that he'd countermanded their father, on top of being the sort of man who couldn't stomach competition from women.

"Then we'll have to assure you are the one to win," Alyx replied, with considerable determination. "Your wife is through there, seeing to her Familiar." She cast him a sidelong look. "I don't wish to question my king, but you're certain this is wise—a foreign sorceress as Queen of the Destrye?"

One day people would stop asking him that. "Yes." He loaded all of his conviction into the affirmation. "More than wise. Oria will be the saving of our people."

Alyx nodded, very seriously. "Then I will serve her and guard her with my life."

She strode off, no doubt to share the news with one and all—which made him realize he'd better tell his mother before she heard it from someone else. He itched to see Oria, to reassure himself of her well-being and bask in her loveliness, but he owed this duty to his mother and the throne.

Which would be her morning room? East side of the house, assuredly, but behind which door? He'd hate to trespass by opening the wrong one. Fortunately—perhaps guided by Arill—Vycayla emerged just then from a room across the hall. Expression set in austere lines of thought, she looked older in the harsh light of morning. The silver threaded thick through her hair, or maybe it showed more because she had it braided back from her face, now that she'd finished dazzling her visitors by playing avatar of the goddess by wearing it long and loose.

She caught sight of him, and her face smoothed into serene lines, making him second-guess that he'd seen signs of age at all. "You're looking much better," she said by way of greeting.

"Your Oria says you slept long and hard."

"I did. Thank you for the healing."

She waved a hand. "Nothing I wouldn't do for the least of humanity—or the animal kingdoms. We treat all who come here, regardless of station or relation."

He set his teeth, ignoring the dig. "I've decided to countermand my father's edict. Women warriors will be welcome in whatever capacity they wish to serve."

Vycayla gave him an impenetrable look, the bright winter light casting sharp shadows under her silver-threaded brows and broad cheekbones. "A bit late," she finally said.

"I can't change the past, Mother. All I can do is change the present."

She nodded, pressing her lips together and looking into some internal vision, a dark reverie he hesitated to interrupt, though it stretched out uncomfortably long. Finally she raised her gaze to his. "Did he… say anything? A message for me, maybe."

His heart stuttered, clenching hard. Had no one told her? He supposed he should've been the one to do it. When he'd returned from Bára, thinking the war over, he'd thrown himself into the pressing problems of assuming kingship—and making sure the Destrye could survive the coming winter. His mother always knew what went on in Dru, with people loyal to her keeping her informed. All his life, Vycayla had known everything before anyone else, and he'd grown accustomed to that reality, relied on that assumption. But, had he been thinking, he would've taken the few days to journey to see his mother and tell her of her husband's and sons' deaths himself.

He'd learned that compassion since marrying Oria, understanding how the widowed spouse would feel in a way that his self of only half a year before hadn't been capable of. Now he had to find a way to give her a truth she could live with.

"It happened too fast for last words or messages," he told his mother. On impulse he picked up her hands, holding them in his. Strong and long-fingered, the bones more pronounced than he remembered. With some surprise in her eyes, his mother gazed back, clearly braced for the pain. "The Trom touched him and he died instantly. I doubt Father—or Ion—even realized their deaths were at hand."

She nodded, swallowing hard, her gray eyes shining with unshed tears. "Not a bad way to die, all in all."

"No." He cleared his throat. Tempting to make something up, to tell her that she'd been in his Father's thoughts, in Ion's, but they'd been focused on the war. If they'd thought of her, they hadn't said. "I'm sorry," he said instead, "that I haven't been a better son, that I blamed you for leaving. I'd like to do better."

Carefully, braced to be rebuffed, he put his arms around his mother, as he hadn't done in easily a decade, surprised to find her shorter and frailer than he remembered. Nothing like Oria's delicate and birdlike bone structure, but far from the hearty mother of his childhood. She leaned into him, returning the embrace, then drew back and framed his face with her hands.

"You have always been a good son," she said. "And you'll be a good king. I've regretted not being a part of your life. I'd like that to change."

"Then you'll stay in Arill City?"

"No," she replied firmly, dashing those hopes. "The Destrye cannot have two queens." She looked past him and he turned to see Oria in the doorway. Wearing a borrowed white robe, Oria looked like an angel of Arill, her copper hair full of light as if touched by the goddess.

"How is Chuffta?" he asked her, and she shook her head, mouth set in unhappy lines.

"He still hasn't woken up." Her gaze went to Vycayla. "Are you sure there's nothing else I can do?"

"Nothing that I know of, child," Vycayla answered with professional compassion. "I've done all I can for him. The ways of the derkesthai are mysterious. I think we must simply wait."

"Is there anyone who would know more?" Oria persisted, her eyes hard and intent. Not one to back down easily from any challenge. His mother might see Oria as a child—and his wife was young in many ways—but she possessed a will of steel.

Vycayla glanced at him and he gave a small shrug. Oria deserved the truth, whatever it might be. "There's a colony of derkesthai," his mother conceded, "two days journey from here, in the Taal mountains. That's why I've seen them, from time to time. You could take your Familiar to them if he hasn't awakened by the time you return."

"Return?" Oria looked at him blankly and Lonen winced internally. Terrible timing.

"From the duel and securing the throne," Vycayla explained slowly, sliding him a look as if she'd begun to doubt Oria's intelligence. Or sanity.

"Oh." Color flooded Oria's face and she clasped her hands together. "I see. There's not enough time to visit the colony before the seven days are up. Of course."

"Precisely," Vycayla agreed. "But I can keep your Familiar here. He'll be safe and warm, in good hands, until you can return and make the journey. If he hasn't woken on his own by then."

Sensitive to the nuances in his mother's assurances, Lonen gave her a hard look. "And the odds that he'll die before we return?"

Oria pressed her fingers to her mouth as if she could take back the sound of distress she'd made.

His mother gave him a resigned glare. "I have no way to evaluate that. We don't have any way to feed him, but he's also partly a magical creature."

"If we left today, that gives us half a day of travel, all of tomorrow, then half a day to the derkesthai colony. Less if we ride fast." He calculated in his head, picturing the map. "Then we could take the diagonal back to Arill City and be back before sunset on the seventh day."

"That's in good weather, and without problems," Vycayla argued. "You'd be cutting it too close."

"Buttercup is faster than most horses," he replied, still in deep thought.

His mother made a choking sound. "Excuse me?"

"My horse." He frowned at her. "You know he's fast—with great endurance."

"I know *that*," she replied, a smile tugging at her stern mouth. "But not that you'd named him *Buttercup*."

"He named himself," Oria inserted with a frown on Buttercup's behalf. "I simply asked what it was. Lonen didn't know before that. I'm surprised a healer of your ability who can look into the wounds of others wouldn't respect the names we choose for ourselves."

Vycayla raised her brows. "Extraordinary." Then returned to Lonen with a firm stare. "It's too risky. You have no idea what they're up to in your absence."

"If you traveled there with your retinue ahead of us, you could affirm my continued good health, suss out the situation, and forestall Rhiten Robson from declaring me dead."

"With Nolan agitating otherwise?" she scoffed.

"You can back him down if necessary. He's as afraid of you as I am."

Vycayla snorted at that. "This is a very bad plan. Needlessly asking for trouble. Are you sure this isn't about sentiment," she said, sliding a glance at Oria, "rather than solid judgment?"

As he wasn't all at sure that his fundamental determination to hold the throne against Nolan's challenge didn't stem more from sentiment than solid judgment in the first place, he couldn't provide a good answer to that. He seemed to have only sentiment left, as nothing made sense the way it used to. Besides which, a large part of him believed that Arill had guided his footsteps to taking Oria as his wife and queen—if the goddess wanted him on the throne of Dru, She'd grace their travels, too. Perhaps Arill Herself had arranged events so they'd visit the derkesthai colony—who could say?

Ultimately, however, Oria watched him with such hope and terror in her eyes that he couldn't possibly make any other choice. So be it.

"Oria needs her Familiar to work her magic," he embroidered on the truth, willing Oria to go along. "I can't win the duel without her, and she can't assist without him. We must do this."

Oria nodded, carefully, though she lowered her gaze to hide her troubled expression.

"Ah, well, that settles it," Vycayla agreed, dusting her hands together, then ringing a bell. "I'll have supplies assembled for you. At least with visiting the colony, if they can't help this one—or if they decide to keep him there—you can choose another Familiar."

Turning to the lady who came to her summons, Vycayla missed Oria's outraged reaction. Lonen gave her what he hoped was a quelling stare, going to her to set a hand on her rigid back. "Let's go pack up our things. The sooner we depart, the better."

Oria flashed him a wry and grateful look. "I couldn't agree more."

"THANK YOU," ORIA said quietly once they were alone in their rooms. "I know you're risking a great deal by doing this."

He gave her a smile as he retrieved the saddlebags. "I promised to do everything in my power to make you happy. Chuffta's well-being is critical to that."

"Even so, I appreciate it." Then she held out her hand, palm up, a determined and expectant look on her face. He scrutinized her empty hand, then raised a questioning brow. "The key to the cabinet where you put Tania's mask, please," she said. A definite command, though at least she added the pleasantry.

"Oria," he began, thinking fast. Not fast enough, as she'd planned this.

"I'm abiding by the rules you set. I didn't argue when you locked it away and hid the key as if I'm a child who can't be trusted."

"Should I point out that you broke that trust only yester-day?"

"But not since. I didn't touch it last night without you and I didn't take the key and open the cabinet while you slept, though I saw in your mind where you hid it."

"You see my thoughts that clearly?" And here he'd worked so hard to cover that.

She smiled slightly. "Things you feel strongly about I see the most clearly. And the mask is amplifying my abilities. You kept worrying about that key and me finding it, even in your dreams."

He didn't know quite what to say to that. He'd known she could read his thoughts and feelings when he married the sorceress. That didn't prevent the revelations from unsettling him, though he had nothing to hide from her. Not anymore, anyway.

"I know you're afraid, Lonen." She closed the distance between them, laying her hands on his chest over his shirt. Tipping her head back, she gave him a long, solemn look, her gorgeous eyes large in her pale face, her lush lips, so torturously kissable and unattainable, slightly parted as she searched for words. "I'm afraid, too. The mask is powerful and I do lose myself in it, more than I've confided in you."

Neither of them was wearing gloves, or he would've put his hands over hers. Instead he ended up waving them in the air. "Then why under Arill's gaze do you—"

"For the same reason you took me to Odymesen's Chapel in the first place," she interrupted in a sharp tone. "I need that mask. More important, I need to learn to work with it—and you need to learn to help me. If we're going to be taking this side trip, that means a lot of hard riding. I might as well use the time productively. Especially since you'll be right there, to supervise." Her mouth quirked with wry impatience as she said it.

"You're giving in, just like that?" Arill forgive him for doubting Oria's sincerity, but... "You're suddenly happy to let me control your access to the mask."

"No, I'm not happy about it," she snapped, eyes flashing with fiery arrogance that perversely reassured him. That was his Oria. "But I also didn't like passing out while I bled from ears, eyes, and nose. So, yes, I'm giving in. You and I are a team. You've said it often enough. I'm going to trust you to take care of me—and see to it that I learn to use the mask without losing myself to it."

"Is this about Chuffta?" he asked her, hesitant to compel her with that kind of debt.

"No. And also yes. You're a good husband to me, Lonen." She smiled ruefully. "I'm trying to be a better wife. Not an irretrievably stubborn one. If that means working with your concerns regarding the mask, then fine."

His heart turned over and he wanted to kiss her with the desperation of a drowning man gasping for air. "You are the best of all possible wives, Oria," he told her, giving himself the weak substitute of running a hand over her shining hair, silky from the washing. "I love you with everything in me, and more than anything else in this world."

"I love you, too," she replied, though a faint line formed between her brows. "We'll get you back to Arill City in time to knock that odious Nolan on his ass, so you can get to the business of being the king you should be."

He didn't tell her he wasn't sure he cared that much about being king. Instead he dug the key out of his pocket and handed it to her. When her eyes sparkled in anticipation, he sent a prayer to Arill that he hadn't made the wrong decision.

~ 9 ~

ORIA ADJUSTED THE fur-wrapped bundle of the sleeping Chuffta. One of Vycayla's many assistants had contrived the sling from the ones women used for carrying recently delivered infants home again. It looped over her shoulders and kept him safely cuddled against her under her fur cloak, while leaving her hands free.

And, thanks to the successful negotiation with Lonen, she now had the mask to use at her discretion—though for now she kept it safely wrapped in its own bag. Time enough to answer its dark siren call. That was a good sign, wasn't it? That she could bide her time before tasting the powerful rush of that magic again. Her arguments had been sound and logical or she wouldn't have been able to convince Lonen. He was far more rational than she was, especially about the mask.

She *had* to learn to use it. So much better this way, that Lonen had agreed.

He stood off to the side, speaking with Vycayla, so Oria checked on Chuffta—for the umpteenth time—parting the furs to peek at him. He did look so much better. Vycayla had splinted his wings and stitched up the bites, bandaging him in places. She'd worked her healing magic on him, too, so that he wasn't even bruised. He might be only sleeping, if not for the utter lack of his presence in her mind.

She couldn't think about that too closely, as scrutinizing that aching empty hole sent flutters of panic through her. The evening before, when she'd found herself alone—and acutely lonely—she'd distracted herself with the mask. Then, when Lonen took it from her, she'd distracted herself with him. Fortunately sex with Lonen worked nearly as well, almost as hypnotically seductive as the mask's magic.

"Farewell, Oria," Vycayla called. "Swift journeys and may Arill bless your endeavors."

Oria lifted a gloved hand in acknowledgement. It was a graceful and generous thing to say, but Oria couldn't yet shed the fury over Vycayla callously suggesting she replace Chuffta with another derkesthai. She'd nearly suggested Vycayla replace her dead son with another, but had bit back those cruel words.

Vycayla didn't understand. None of the Destrye could, really, and Oria had to remind herself of that reality. Even in Bára, no one else had been paired with a derkesthai Familiar in generations, not since Oria's great-grandmother. Oria only received Chuffta because her mother had journeyed to a colony when Oria turned seven. Queen Rhianna had recognized Oria's unusual sensitivity to magic and had known her precocious daughter would need a Familiar to help her through the difficult trials life would hold for her—as Rhianna's own grandmother had.

Oria frowned to herself, thinking back as Lonen embraced Vycayla. Queen Rhianna had said something more before Oria and Lonen fled Bára, something about how Oria would need Chuffta's help in other ways—much as Lonen had said when he lied to his mother about the duel.

Maybe it hadn't been such an untruth. Of everyone around her, Lonen understood her relationship with—and dependence on—Chuffta better than anyone. That was part of why she'd made the concession on him controlling the mask, because her husband did love her. He was risking reclaiming his throne to help her with Chuffta, after all.

She'd simply have to give her utmost to do the same for him. They would make it back in time, he'd win the duel, and then she'd give everything she had to securing Dru and the Destrye for him. Even if it killed her.

Using the mask very well might, but it would be worth it. That part she wouldn't tell him, however.

Lonen mounted behind her. "Buttercup looks sound. How's he feeling?"

She patted the warhorse's shoulder and he pranced in place. "Like a foal again, he says."

Lonen laughed. "I thought he doesn't use words."

"He doesn't. I'm approximating the translation." She glanced over her shoulder at him, always happy to hear his laughter. So she caught his change of expression as he focused past her.

Turning to see what struck him so, she took in the six women in battle gear like Lonen had worn back in the attack on Bára, riding horses laden with packs and weapons. The one leading, with black curling hair in braids on each side of her head, and snapping dark eyes, bowed in the saddle. "Your Highnesses."

"What is this, Alyx?" Lonen asked.

"We're your escort and honor guard," she replied very seriously. "Lest you be outnumbered by the wildlife again," she added, a cheeky sparkle in her eyes.

"You humble me," he said in a dry tone.

Alyx sobered. "With all due respect, my king, my queen," she nodded to Oria, seeming to mean it, "we're all volunteers, committed to seeing you healthy and ruling Dru, no matter what you may face."

"I suppose you do have a personal stake," he observed.

They inclined their heads. "That's how it should be, yes?" Alyx replied. "We give our all to support the crown that supports us and who we are."

Wondering what prompted all that—and the women's emotions, riding so high and full of fervor, she sensed it from that distance—and raised a brow at Lonen.

"I'll explain later," he muttered. "Then let's be off. The wolves await!"

HAVING THE WOMEN warriors along turned out to be both a blessing and a hindrance. Lonen relaxed some of his tense vigilance, no longer solely in charge of their safety. Oria couldn't openly handle the mask, knowing without discussing it that Lonen preferred to keep the existence of the mask, and their possession of it, a secret. They couldn't banter with each other, but also they couldn't argue.

And Oria could discreetly experiment with grien without Lonen interrogating her.

Communing with the mask reminded her in some ways of touching the vast pool of sgath the priestesses had generated back in Bára. Oria had grown up in constant contact with it, so that sgath had been familiar, even soothing. Each of Bára's sister cities had their own reserves of sgath, pulled from the wild magic and made coherent by the meditative efforts of that city's priestesses. Oria had been forced to flee before ascending to the ranks where the arcane process was taught, but it involved the application of *hwil*, to remove the taint of emotion, of the violence of nature, to purify the magic for consumption by the priests.

Naturally, Oria knew even less about how the men wielded their grien magic. They took in the sgath—unable to produce it on their own—and transformed it into active magic according to their own skills and natural talents. Each priest employed his grien magic in a preferred modality, whether manifesting earthquakes or fireballs.

Or creating golems to attack their neighbors.

As a woman, Oria shouldn't have been able to manifest grien. When the temple discovered she could, even though she'd legitimately beaten her brother Yar in her own duel for the throne, they'd declared her a monster, anathema, and exiled her.

However, as Chuffta had pointed out, why would the temple outlaw something that wasn't possible? Clearly a woman *could* wield grien magic, like a man could, because Oria did. Whoever had created that law must've known of the possibility, but considered the ability a dangerous one. Even more than summoning the devastatingly powerful and destructive Trom, as Yar had done. Difficult to believe, as that summoning corrupted Yar visibly from his first attempt.

She shivered at the memory of Yar's eyes turning matte black like the Trom's. He'd tried to hide them behind his priest's mask, but she'd seen them. Just as she'd seen herself in nightmares, with the same inhuman gaze.

That wouldn't happen to her, though, as she'd never summon the vile Trom—or touch that magic in any way. Oria was different, and she'd trust to that difference to protect her. Or did that difference doom her? Her mother had asked the derkesthai for a volunteer to be her daughter's Familiar because of her unusual nature. The Trom had known something about her, calling her Ponen, an old word that meant potential, her mother had explained. But potential for what?

Corruption, certainly. The mask held that, too. When she'd first touched it, back at the tomb, the magic stored in the artifact had felt inert, motionless as a frozen river. But like ice melting in proximity to warmth, the mask's magic had thawed over the last day in her possession. More and more it seemed to reach out to her, begging to be used.

Wanting to be worn.

She would only wear it as a last resort, however. Not only because Lonen would loathe seeing it on her—and very possibly do something extreme, like try to destroy it. She also wasn't sure what it would do to her to actually wear it. No, she'd save it for the point of no return, because every instinct in her screamed that once she took that step, there would be no coming back from it.

You've taken not one, but several steps farther down your path, the Trom had said to her in a dream so real she'd nearly suffocated before Lonen managed to wake her. That warning no doubt reinforced the fatalistic sense that she wouldn't come back from this course of action.

One thing was certain: she had only herself in this. No one could teach her. She'd have to learn through trial—and hope the errors didn't destroy her.

At least, not before she destroyed Yar.

Thinking back through all she knew about magic—male and female—and what she'd learned about using her own, she slipped one finger inside the bag, not touching the polished metal directly, but over the layers Lonen had wrapped it in.

Missing nothing, Lonen threaded his arm inside her cloak, winding it securely around her waist—not for support so much as to remind her that he'd been paying attention would be watching her closely.

Fine. Spinning her resentment into gratitude would be an exercise, like transmuting sgath into grien.

Before, when she'd opened herself to the mask's magic, it had overwhelmed her, like the bore tides of Bára, coming in an unstoppable rush, so fast that a horse couldn't outrun the drowning waves. That would be the first step, to manage the flow and control it. Even if that seemed as unlikely as standing before a tidal wave and holding up her hands, asking it politely to stay back.

Intention mattered. Her mother had always said that, as had her teachers. *What people believe becomes real. Don't put attention on a result you do not want.*

So instead of seeing the mask's magic as an irresistible wave, she pictured it as a slow trickle, a soothing sip of water from a cup. Carefully, she drank from the mental glass.

"Ouch!" Oria batted at Lonen's hand, pinching a fold of skin at her hip painfully.

"Had to bring you back," he explained in a rough voice, changing his grip to a soothing caress over the likely bruised skin.

"By pinching me?"

"You didn't answer when I spoke to you and I didn't want to alert our companions that anything was amiss," he explained quietly in her ear.

Up ahead, Alyx led the way, scanning the forest while two other women behind her chatted amiably. Another pair rode behind Buttercup, with the sixth woman at the rear.

Oria sighed. "I see your point. How long was I unresponsive?"

"That I could discern, about fifteen minutes."

And it had felt like only seconds to her. All right then, a drop of water, rather than a sip. "I'll see if I can sample a smaller amount of the magic."

"Oria..."

"Lonen. Look, no blood." She showed him her face, smiling.

He sighed heavily, his chest rising and falling against her back. "Point taken. Go ahead. But I don't like this."

"You'll like it when Dru and the Destrye are safe."

"Not without you," he muttered, but said nothing more, so she let it go.

Once again, she opened her magical senses to the mask, but this time imagining tasting the smallest drop, like the jewelbirds delicately sampling the blossoms on her rooftop back in Bára, before the garden dried up and blew away. At the same time, she did her best to keep awareness of the physical world around her. The low conversation of the women warriors, the crunch of horse hooves on the snow, the scent of mountain air and the soap Lonen had used, his arm warm and strong around her waist and Chuffta a soft weight in the sling around her neck. She kept her eyes closed, the better to focus on the image of sipping that sweet magical nectar—neither sgath nor wild magic, but something else entirely, nourishing and invigorating.

It filled her with a vitality she hadn't felt since leaving Bára—and very carefully she closed off contact again. "How was that?" she asked.

"I didn't notice anything," Lonen replied carefully. "I didn't try to talk to you, but you didn't go inert either, like you did before."

"Good." Excellent, really. "Now I'm going to try something."

"What will you do?" he sounded wary.

She didn't know. "I want to see if I can do something with it."

"Grien magic?"

"Yes—and no. The mask magic isn't exactly sgath, so I'm thinking the active aspect won't be exactly grien. Does that make sense?"

She felt him nod slowly. "Sure."

Something in his tone made her laugh. "You mean, as much as anything to do with Báran magic makes sense?"

He shifted around her, his breath warm against her temple. "You make sense, my sexy sorceress. That's all that matters." Then he murmured several naughty suggestions for how she might use her magic.

Blushing, she cast a glance at the women riding in front of them, though she and Lonen had been speaking too quietly for them to overhear. It said something, that she worried more about them hearing Lonen's flirtations than their discussion of magic.

And yet... he provided a sort of balance to her efforts. The earthiness of Lonen's strong body wrapped around her, along with the vivid images of what they could do together, helped to ground her in the face of the out-of-body disconnectedness the mask's magic created. It helped anchor her in that flood of enticing power. Maybe he'd been right to push her to share this experimentation with him—though he couldn't possibly have predicted this.

"I was thinking something more applicable to, say, dueling or battling the Trom," she informed him tartly, wriggling to back him off.

Lonen laughed amiably and gave her room. "I like my idea better, but go ahead. Just try not to startle the horses."

Wouldn't that be wonderful? She could panic their little caravan and send them in all directions, possibly off the precipice to their deaths. Biting her lip, she hummed in uncertainty.

"Don't worry so much," Lonen said in her ear. "I was just lightening the mood. These are all well-trained horses that won't panic easily. And it's good for you to learn to project magic away from your own people, right? Think of it as an exercise in that kind of control, too."

She nodded, somewhat reassured, though not completely. It would be ideal to practice where she couldn't hurt anyone, but then all of her attempts to use her magic—all her life—had been fraught with difficulty. She would never have the ideal situation she'd once dreamed of, some perfect day when she'd have easy mastery of *hwil*, receive her own mask certifying her as a real priestess, and then be admitted to some vast trove of information that would enable her to know everything and resolve all her doubts forever.

It had been a childish idea of what being a priestess would be like. Somewhere along the way—starting with the realization that no one understood what *hwil* should feel like any better than she did—she'd begun to understand that the powerful sorcerers and sorceresses of Bára were making things up as they went along. No one lived free of doubts and no one possessed all the answers.

Magic came from the world around them, a force as powerful as drought or blizzards or bore tides… or packs of wolves. Maybe it wasn't reasonable to think about controlling the world, forcing it into obedience. Yar saw things that way, and she would do everything not to follow his example. She might instead work with nature, coaxing it along and directing the course of things.

The sorcerers had loved to use grien in loud and destructive ways—but they were men and that fit with how they did most everything. She hadn't grown up with three brothers not understanding that much.

Oria had used her own grien in various ways back in Bára, when she'd been replete with magic—blasting doors open and creating a physical "touch" that affected Lonen. Thus his salacious suggestions. But she'd also brought blooming, fruiting life to dying plants. And grown vines out of stone at the trials. She could communicate with Buttercup and sense thoughts and emotions from people. And Lonen had said she'd made the forest inhale, then blown the wolves over.

"Oria?" Lonen stroked her arm.

"Yes."

"Just checking."

She laughed. "Thinking, not disappearing." She focused on the trees lining the path, how they felt to her. Back in Arill City, she'd held a leaf and sensed the life force in it, its connectedness to the tree it had fallen from, and to the trees that had been its neighbors, the forest overall. Holding that feeling in her mind, she poured a bit of magic into it, imagining a tree up ahead shrugging off its blanket of snow.

Unfortunately, she did startle the horses. At least, Alyx's steed jumped, then danced sideways, ears pointed at the tree that suddenly dropped snow, whoomfing down and sending sparkles of ice through the air.

All of the fighters had their weapons in hand and pointed at the tree and the area around it, warily searching for the cause of the disturbance. All except Lonen, who laughed silently behind her, shaking as he muffled the sound.

When their escort decided no imminent danger presented itself, they moved on. "Well done," Lonen murmured. "It will be very useful to dump snow on the heads of our enemies."

"Don't sweep sand at me," she hissed back. "I wanted something small."

"I know, love. I'm just teasing."

"I know." And she smiled, well pleased with herself. It had worked just as she'd envisioned. A small feat, yes, but also neatly controlled—nearly unprecedented for her. Shaking the tree had only required a bit of magic, too, so she needn't sip more. That would be her protocol for herself: maintain her magical stores without overloading, and apply active magic with precision.

She began to believe they might triumph after all.

~ 10 ~

L ONEN MADE A game of observing as Oria practiced her magic in subtle ways, teaching himself to recognize what occurred naturally and what was due to her sorcerous nudging. He did it in part because it gave him something to do. Having Alyx and her warriors along relieved him of the need to scrutinize every sound or flicker of shadow—but he also needed to remain alert. The residual sleepiness from the extensive healing beckoned him to doze, which he couldn't allow. Focusing his attention on Oria, trying to feel her subtle magical shifts, and predicting what she might try next kept him occupied without distracting him entirely.

Also, he wanted to hone his ability to know where *her* attention was. If they were to work together in a productive partnership that would allow her to use the mask without becoming the monster he feared—and would possibly have to destroy, if it didn't kill her first—then understanding how she wielded her magic would be key. As they traveled through the short afternoon and into the early nightfall, he paid attention to when she'd fallen into the mask-induced trances, how long they lasted, and signs that she'd emerged.

He got good at spotting the twigs that curled like fingers, or the flocks of birds that rose from the canopy and then flew in sculpted formations before dispersing. He refrained from teasing her—much—though the sound of her amusement and tart rejoinders reassured him that she remained the woman he knew, and hadn't been taken over by whatever ruthless force occupied the mask.

They made it to a cabin Alyx knew a few hours after dark. Another reason he appreciated that she and her troop had chosen to accompany them. He vaguely knew of the ridge of mountains that his mother had indicated housed the derkesthai colony, but he'd never been there. He certainly wouldn't have known the location of the cabins stocked with supplies for travelers going this direction. He and Oria might've gotten lucky, but they were trusting to fortune enough as it was.

Alyx and her women seemed invested in proving themselves, too, insisting that he and Oria take their ease while the rest of them got the fires going and cooked food. He had to admit, the perks of being king made situations like this far more comfortable.

Oria sat by the fireplace, tending to Chuffta as Vycayla had demonstrated. The derkesthai seemed to sleep as deeply as ever, but his limbs and joints moved easily enough as Oria gently manipulated them, rubbing oil into his scaled hide to keep it supple. Lonen found himself missing the derkesthai's antics. Chuffta would've loved to help tend the fire. He could only imagine how much more Oria must grieve over the lizard's injured state, though she'd said little about it. Neither of them did, somewhat superstitiously avoiding the topic.

Now, however, he crouched beside her where she sat on the hearth, legs curled beneath her and Chuffta on his blanket before her. "Any changes?" he asked, choosing the question carefully.

She shook her head, lovingly petting her Familiar, as if her touch could heal. "He seems weirdly the same, like he's some kind of doll and not a living creature at all anymore."

Lonen frowned to himself, making sure he didn't show his worry. "Well, derkesthai are magical creatures, yes? Maybe they don't react like other animals or people."

She glanced up at him, eyes opaque. "I hadn't thought of it that way. But as we were riding and I was *practicing*..." She lowered her voice so none of the others could overhear. "I worked at listening to other minds—yours, Buttercup's, the other horses, birds in the trees."

"What about the other Destrye?" he asked.

Oria shrugged a little. "I made an effort not to. It seemed like too much an invasion of privacy."

"But you don't mind invading mine?" he pressed, deliberately frowning at her now.

Her mouth fell open, a look of distress on her face. "Lonen, I—oh! You..." She narrowed her eyes and sudden dizziness assailed him, tipping him onto his ass.

Blinking in surprise, he took in her merry smile. "That was you? Well done."

She glanced around, but the others weren't paying attention to them, rather studiously giving them privacy. "Thank you. And no, you have no privacy from me. That way I'll know if you look too long at the pretty Destrye ladies."

"If you've looked in my mind, you know I have eyes only for you, love."

She blushed, making it clear she had a very good idea of the sorts of things he thought about where Oria was concerned, then looked again at Chuffta. "I wish we could get there sooner. Where *are* these Taal Mountains? It seems like we're only going into colder winter, not somewhere..."

"Warmer?" he filled in, crossing his legs and sitting more comfortably. "I wondered about that, too. But the Taal

Mountains have a lot of volcanic activity, which would provide a lot of heat for a colony of derkesthai. Isn't that where Queen Rhianna went when she recruited Chuffta for you?"

"She never said," Oria murmured. "She was… vague about a lot of things to do with him."

"Maybe this will be an opportunity for you to get answers then," he offered with a smile.

"Do we even know how to approach them, what to say?" she asked.

He shook his head, keeping the smile in place. "My mother hasn't been there. She's seen them fly and she's studied some about them. But she said you have to be invited into the colony itself. They have considerable ability to defend themselves, as you might imagine."

Oria's brows forked with concern. "Why didn't you tell me that—how are we supposed to get an invitation?"

He shrugged cheerfully. "My mother figured you'd be able to, since you're bound to one of them. Surely they'll recognize and admit you, if only because you bring Chuffta with you."

"So much that's not certain," she murmured, stroking Chuffta's rounded belly, then looking at him, her gaze troubled. "I hope this side trip won't be a gigantic waste of time and effort. We're risking a great deal by doing this, and might gain nothing from it."

"No sense trying to change the direction of the arrow once it's loosed from the bow," he replied firmly. "And we may gain a great deal from it. Remember—Arill is guiding us."

Oria made a face. "I will never understand how you can put so much store in a goddess you don't even know exists."

"It's the barbarian way," he answered cheerfully. "Besides, I put store in you and you are very, very real."

THEY LEFT EARLY the following morning and traveled fast with few breaks, making better time than predicted. Alyx pushed them on to a more distant cabin and, despite the late night, they rose at dawn, arriving at the derkesthai colony after only a couple of hours' ride. It was the morning of the fifth day after Nolan had issued his challenge, and two days' hard riding from there to make it back in time.

Ah well. It would be what it would be.

As his mother had promised, Lonen easily recognized the landscape as their destination. Steam rose from pools of unnaturally colored liquids—oranges swirling with red and pink, and greens as luminescent as Chuffta's flame. If the steam rising thick in the chilly morning air, shrouding the landscape in stinking fog, wasn't evidence enough of the intense heat under the ground, the barren rock terrain with no snow cover proved it. Indeed, as their horses picked their way along the narrow trail—a path they'd been repeatedly warned not to deviate from, lest they fall through a thin crust masquerading as solid ground—heavy snow began to fall. The downy, wet flakes that quickly whitened Buttercup's black mane disappeared as they hit the ground, leaving no sign that they'd fallen. Lonen fancied that he'd hear the hiss of them burning from ice to steam if not for the pervasive popping and bubbling noises the virulently colored pools made.

With the snowfall the fog thickened even more, growing so dense that Lonen could barely see Buttercup's ears, much less the horse ahead of them on the trail.

Oria made a surprised sound, startling a little in his arms.

"What's wrong?" he asked. He hadn't meant to whisper. There was no reason to, but something about the hush of fog and sinister bubbles had him feeling as if they walked into an ambush.

"I hear them," Oria replied, just as quietly. "Lonen—there are so many of them! Lots of minds, a chorus of derkesthai voices."

"Talking to you?"

"No—to each other. I'm not sure they're aware of us yet. It's more like hearing birdsong in the forest."

She sounded rapt and wondering, and for a brief moment he envied her the ability to hear those inaudible voices. He'd only heard Chuffta's mind-voice at the oasis in the desert, when something about the magic there had allowed it. "Can you tell what they're talking about?"

Making a little sound of impatience, she shrugged. "It's like trying to hear one conversation in a vast feast hall where everyone is chattering. I can pick out words here and there, phrases sometimes, but nothing that—aha! They've noticed us."

"Incoming," Alyx called at the same moment. "Stay alert."

"Treat them as friendly unless I say otherwise," Lonen called. "Oria will talk to them."

"I don't like being on this narrow trail," Alyx replied grimly.

"Stay on it," he ordered. "No matter what. The price for deviating is too high."

"They're here," Oria said, and the rhythmic whoomph of wings in the thick air approached them.

Bright green points showed through the fog first, then the slightly darker white bodies in the swirling fog. Three of them hovered before Oria, bobbing in the mist, the one at the leading point of their triangle easily three times as big as Chuffta. It seemed they shouldn't be able to hover like that—certainly not with their wings beating no faster than a relaxed heartbeat—but he let it go. He had no idea how a living creature could breathe burning flame, and yet he'd seen it.

Perhaps one day, when he and Oria had lived long lives together, and produced sorcerous children, he'd be accustomed to the strangeness of magic and the things it wrought.

"We greet you," Oria said aloud, for his benefit and the others, as she could speak to them directly mind-to-mind if she chose. "May I present His Highness King Lonen of Dru, the human name for the lands on which you dwell." She paused, the lull filled with a hiss of escaping steam from something hidden in the fog.

"I am Oria, late of Bára, and now a denizen of Dru, married to Lonen."

One of the horses stamped, blowing out breath through its lips, restless at the halt. Not Buttercup, who remained steadfast and still.

"In time that may be so," Oria replied. "I'm sure His Highness will be happy to entertain negotiations. But we have pressing matters at the moment that—"

She shifted, glancing at him over her shoulder, a meaningful look he couldn't interpret. "I understand," she said, speaking to them again. "I apologize if I offered insult. Of course we will discuss it now. I am clumsy in the ways of derkesthai etiquette."

To his surprise, she laughed then, a delighted giggle. "It's true that Chuffta is not the most discreet of ambassadors." She pushed back her cloak, unbuckling the sling carrying her Familiar against her breast, then unfolded the furs to reveal his quiet form. One of the derkesthai behind the leader zoomed forward, abruptly landing on Lonen's knee, while the other two flew off into the mist. Their visitor, only about twice Chuffta's size, folded its wings with a clap, and dug in. He thanked Arill that he wore thick leather, though he still had to steel himself not to flinch—and that Buttercup knew Chuffta well. Even an unflappable warhorse might be expected to shy under such circumstances.

Given the potential death trap around them, that eventuality became especially daunting.

Oria had fallen silent as the derkesthai examined Chuffta. It bent over the unconscious Familiar, studying him, sniffing, flicking out a forked tongue to taste, and even using the nimble thumbs at the wing tips to prod him. It looked up at Oria finally, and they communed for another long space of silence. Buttercup flicked his ears, betraying the impatience he sensed in Lonen to know the verdict. Lonen clamped down on his frustration. The warhorse was far too sensitive to his subconscious signals. But Lonen really hated waiting. And not knowing.

Oria made a choked sound and he risked leaning around for a glimpse of her face. Silent tears tracked down her pallid skin, her lips on the violet side of their usual pink, from the cold—and perhaps chilling grief. Still she remained locked in silent conversation with the strange derkesthai, and he knew Oria wouldn't appreciate an interruption. Possibly not the derkesthai—who very saliently still had talons gripping Lonen's thigh—either.

An exercise in restraint, then.

Finally, and blessedly, the derkesthai released its pinching grip and took off with another startling clap of wings, immediately swallowed by the thick fog, and increasing snowfall.

"Oria?" he asked.

"We're to follow," she replied, voice thick with tears.

"Follow what?" Alyx called from ahead. "I can't see an Arill-blessed thing."

Oria sniffed, swallowed hard. "The path."

"I don't like it…" Alyx trailed off, a warning in her voice.

"I can see what they see," Oria said, bundling Chuffta up again. "I'll get down and—"

"Absolutely not," Lonen cut her off. "Alyx—follow the same trail. Oria will let us know if we need to deviate."

"Yes, Your Highness," she replied crisply and neutrally, all doubt and caution gone. The horses moved.

"Tell me," he urged Oria. "Are our worst fears realized—is he lost to us?"

"No. Oh, no," she hastily assured him, then hiccoughed on a small sob. "He is alive, and they think they can bring him out of it."

Relief flooded him, a sweet and clean release of tension he hadn't realized gripped him so hard. "Then why all the tears, love?"

She scrubbed a hand over her face. "Because I did it to him, Lonen. I caused this because I'm a monster. It's time we both faced that reality."

~ 11 ~

NO MORE WEEPING, Oria ordered herself. Tears had never solved a cursed thing. Besides, she was more furious with herself than anything else. Feeling so frisky and clever, playing with manipulating the trees and birds along the way, so certain she'd demonstrate to Lonen once and for all that she could handle this ancient gift that was her legacy.

This revelation proved not only that she didn't know what she was doing, but that she was a profound danger to everything good, decent, and right in the world.

"Explain that statement, Oria," Lonen said, with more stern command this time. "I want to know what that creature said to you."

Tukcha would not appreciate being referred to as "that creature," and she was no doubt still listening in. "Be polite," she hissed. "They can hear us just fine."

"Voice or thoughts?" Lonen asked immediately, his mind clicking over into that orderly and suspicious mode that she thought of as his warlord self. Just as he'd cue Buttercup to go from placid companion to ferocious battle horse, he did the same with himself. From concerned lover to calculating king in a flash. He might not even be aware of it in himself.

Something she could stand to learn from, no doubt, though nothing could prevent her from her terrible destiny.

"Both," she replied, focusing on the immediate question. "The larger the derkesthai, the more … powerful their thought projection and reading." When the colony guardian, Soldano, had spoken in her mind when the three first flew up to them, the sheer volume in his mind-voice had struck her so hard she felt as if she'd been knocked out of the saddle. What a surprise to find herself still atop Buttercup, secure in Lonen's grip. "Tukcha—the one who landed on you and examined Chuffta—is a healer and she said that what I did, back in the forest when the wolves attacked, that I—" Her voice caught, but she used her fury at herself and her idiotic bumbling to burn the weakness away. "I did something that messed up their brains. The wind didn't knock them over. I put them to sleep."

"And Chuffta got caught in it, too."

"Yes." She could feel his relief and guessed the source of it without bothering to track it back. "And yes, I'm grateful also that I didn't accidentally do it to you, too."

"That's not what I was thinking," he chided her gently. "I'm relieved that they can help him. So it's only a question of waking him up?"

He finished on a hopeful note, ever the optimist. Ahead, the fog changed color, darkening as the large mouth of a cavern loomed before them. The horses' hooves clapped with brighter sounds, hitting solid stone instead of the softer path that had wended through the pools. Alyx directed the others softly, distributing the warrior women into a flanking pattern. Not much time left.

"They haven't said exactly what needs to be done to waken him. I have to go in and consult with them."

"I'll go with you," he replied immediately, as she'd known he would.

"No. All of you have to wait out here."

"Not negotiable, Oria. I'm not letting you go in there alone."

"Then you sentence Chuffta to death," she replied, remarkably calm. She might be in a sort of shock. "And we'll have wasted all this time and effort. You'll have put your chances of claiming the throne in jeopardy, and along with it the futures of both our peoples."

"You're more important to me than—"

"No, Lonen. I'm not. Neither of us is allowed the luxury of putting sentiment ahead of duty."

"Isn't that what you're doing now?" he answered in a quiet but harsh voice. She wished she could see his face, but she didn't dare take her eyes off the cavern. From the dark, mist-shrouded maw, white shapes streamed out, flying soundlessly. The Destrye might see them as more fog, but she knew them for hundreds, maybe thousands of derkesthai, spiraling out into an aerial dance, guard and escort.

"You're putting sentiment ahead of your own safety," Lonen continued, oblivious. "I know what Chuffta means to you, but I won't let you put yourself in danger for..." He trailed off, seeing at last. "What in Arill's name is that?" he whispered in hushed awe.

An enormous white derkesthai emerged from the cavern. Or rather, his snout did. Taller than even Vycayla's manor, with green eyes that would be easily Lonen's height, the giant, triangular face pierced the fog. All the horses but Buttercup panicked, rearing and shrieking as their riders cursed. Even Buttercup twitched, a ripple running whole-body through him and he danced a little in place.

One woman fell, hitting the ground with a cry of pain and her horse pivoted to run.

"Best control your steeds," a voice thundered through Oria's mind.

Wincing, Oria quickly reached for the horse's mind, grabbing it first, then gathering the others carefully, like a bouquet of thorny blossoms. First she stilled them, then she calmed them. Too heavy-handed, as the horses hung their heads in lax resignation, as if she'd beaten them into submission. At least she hadn't had to do that to Buttercup.

"At least they won't cook themselves blundering into a hot pool." The mind-voice of the derkesthai king sounded mildly exasperated with her. *"So you are the ponen. And you've broken your Familiar with unrestrained magic. How distressingly careless of you."*

"Oria, what—"

"Shh," she cut Lonen off. "Yes, Great One," she replied aloud, hoping Lonen would take the cue. "I've misused my magic and harmed my Familiar. I bring him here to be healed. Tukcha indicated it might be possible."

"Tukcha is wise, so I defer to her opinion. You will, of course, accompany him so we may determine if you can be taught. But only you may enter, Ponen. These others will leave come nightfall."

"Thank you, Great One," she answered. "The gift of your permission is beyond price. I understand that only I may enter." She went to dismount, but Lonen remained unmoving. He might have been a granite wall for all the luck she'd have budging him if he didn't agree. She twisted to look at him, his face set in ridged and obstinate lines, exactly as she'd pictured in her mind. She laid a gloved hand on his cheek, and his flinty gaze dropped from the derkesthai king to her face. "I have to do this, Lonen."

"I don't like it."

"I know." And he hadn't even heard the worst part. "I have to go alone, because they'll heal Chuffta only if I agree to their lessons in controlling my power."

"You can come back another time and—"

"No." She looked into his eyes, willing him to understand. She couldn't avoid telling him now. "They won't let me leave. I'm a danger, Lonen."

"You're not," he insisted, but underneath his steadfast love and faith in her, she caught the undercurrent of doubt. He'd seen it in her, how very destructive she could become. Because he loved her, he couldn't face it, not entirely.

"We don't have a choice. I need you to let me do this, for Chuffta, for me, because you agreed to trust me."

His expression didn't soften, though something in his eyes changed, making the color less stony. "You ask a great deal of me."

"I always have." It should've been a joke, but it came out as seriously as she felt.

"We've always asked a great deal of each other," he agreed, then managed something like a smile. "Fortunately we're both capable of tremendous greatness, so it's not a problem."

She smiled back, her heart bursting. "I have to do this."

"I know." With a sigh, he swung down from Buttercup and held up his arms to help her down. Setting her on her feet, he kept a hold of her. "Are you taking the mask in with you?" he asked, the very neutrality of his tone scorching her.

She nodded. "I may need it."

"How long will this take?"

"I don't know," she lied. It had sounded like days, maybe longer, in her mind, though the derkesthai didn't track time the same way humans did.

"Are you coming back to me?" He searched her face as he asked the question, somehow reading the evasion in her.

"Of course," she said, infusing her tone and expression with all the certainty she didn't feel.

His eyes flicked to the derkesthai king, who thankfully remained silent. Perhaps he understood how crushing his mind-voice could be. "That's a dragon, Oria."

"Not the same kind as the Trom have."

Lonen gave her a wry look. "In color only. Tell me the truth."

"I'll do everything in my power to come back to you," she promised. "I've made you promises. I've vowed to be your queen. I won't break my word if I can help it."

"Promises and vows," he echoed. "Is that all we have, in the end?"

"We have love. I love you, Lonen." On impulse she slid her hand behind his neck for leverage, stood on tiptoe and pressed her lips to his.

It burned. And it nearly broke her, feeling the depth of heartbreak in him. And the sheer taste of him flooded her, his emotions mirroring hers with bruising force.

He tore her off of him. "Oria!"

"It's all right," she said through blistering lips. "It will heal." And she'd have that reminder, of what it meant to be human, and loved. Resolutely she walked away, the derkesthai king and the thousands of Chuffta's brethren watching with interest.

"Oria..." Lonen called after her, and she turned to see him standing there, one fist clutching Buttercup's reins, the other hand extended toward her. At whatever he saw in her face, he dropped the hand. "We'll be waiting here for you."

"You have to go at the end of the day. You can't spend the

night here. The derkesthai won't let you."

"We'll wait," he replied, implacable.

She stepped into the shadow of the cavern. "If I haven't returned by an hour before nightfall, go back to the cabin where we slept last night."

"What? No."

"You can't sleep out here, and you can't navigate that path in the dark." She glanced at Alyx, who looked both stunned and resolute. "Will you promise me to see that he does as I ask?"

"Yes, Your Highness," Alyx replied grimly, ignoring Lonen's growl of protest. "We'll protect our king, even against his worst impulses, if necessary."

"Thank you." She looked to Lonen again. "And you will leave for Arill City in the morning, whether I'm with you or not."

He made a wordless sound of protest.

"Swear to your goddess that you will," she demanded. "Everything we've gone through will have been for nothing if you don't go claim your throne. Everything I've sacrificed, too. I'll be there to help fight the duel, if I can."

"I can't win without you."

"Of course you can." She summoned a smile. "You always win. That's your nature."

He glared at her, clearly searching for the argument to convince her.

"But you assuredly won't win if you've been declared dead, so you have to get there in time. Delay the duel as long as you can once you're there, but promise me you'll leave the cabin at dawn, no matter what."

"I won't," he ground out. "I'm waiting for you. How can you travel without us?"

"I'll find a way. But swear it now, by Arill, or I won't come at all."

His face went blank. "You would do that to me?"

"Not because I want to. The derkesthai won't let you stay here and I need you to swear you'll journey to Arill City without me, if necessary. I can't concentrate on what I need to do if I'm worried about this."

A muscle bulged in his jaw as he clenched it. "I swear, by Arill's hard heart, that we'll leave for the cabin an hour before sunset, then for Arill City at first light in the morning. Here." He took a pack of food and water that Alyx had been efficiently assembling as they spoke, the warrior woman's mind, as ever, on the practical. "If you're not with us, you'll need provisions. Just in case."

Oria took the bag, closing her eyes in relief, feeling the weight of at least that worry off her shoulders.

"Swear to me," Lonen grated, "that you'll meet me in Arill City."

"I don't believe in your goddess."

"Then on whatever you do hold dear," he snarled, pushed too far.

"I swear on your love then," she said softly, though the stone apron amplified her voice, giving the vow a ringing quality. "On your heart, as that is the most precious thing in all the world to me, that if I have breath in my body, I'll come to you."

She turned and walked into the dark cavern, ignoring the sound of him calling after her. It was the hardest thing she'd ever done in her life.

It was also the first time in her life that she was certain she'd made the right decision.

~ **12** ~

"Looks like we'll be waiting out the rest of the day here," Alyx said, taking command when Lonen didn't. Buttercup's reins bit into his hand where he clutched them in the fist he'd longed to plant in that dragon's snout. It had looked at him so mockingly, and then mentally *leaned* on him. Lonen had never felt anything like that before, like jaws vising on his will, just enough pressure to make it clear it could break him with a thought.

And so he'd just let Oria walk in there, very likely never to return. Even now, as he contemplated going after her, he felt the impossibility of trying. He could no more force his legs to carry him into the cavern than he could pull Grienon from the sky and have the moon for breakfast.

"Breakfast, Your Highness?" One of Alyx's warriors—Fenive, he thought—stood before him. Not uncannily echoing his thoughts, but offering him a plate of food.

He blinked and saw the other women gathered around a campfire, the scent of warm food wafting over. How long had he been standing there, thinking he planned to go after Oria, while instead he'd lost time? Buttercup, released from the vigil, nuzzled him. "Sorry, buddy," he said to the warhorse. "Thank you," he said to Fenive, taking the plate of food, though he didn't feel hungry. He'd long ago learned to eat when he could, to keep his body fueled.

"I'll make your horse comfortable for the wait, Your Highness," Fenive offered. "I already ate."

"Thank you," he repeated, his head still feeling thick. If the Great One—ha, to that title—had affected him like that, he could only guess at how the far more sensitive Oria had felt actually hearing its voice in her head. "This is Buttercup," he said, without thinking, introducing the warhorse so he wouldn't treat Fenive as an enemy.

Fenive raised a dubious brow, taking in the ferocious black stallion. "As you say, Your Highness."

"It's his own name," he explained. "Oria asked him."

He felt extraordinarily foolish, trying to explain the ridiculous name as Oria had done with his mother, but Fenive nodded in understanding. "Queen Oria is a powerful sorceress, indeed." She eased the reins from his hand. "Your Highness," she added, inclining her head as a reminder at the plate he'd forgotten he held.

So he ate. The food helped. He paced awhile as the sun parted the clouds, dispersing the fog. At Alyx's urging, he napped while they stood watch, falling asleep hard, then jerking awake from dreams of Oria dying in dragon fire—the harsh scent scorching his nostrils a breeze from the stinking pools, not her burning hair as he'd so vividly witnessed in nightmares.

Unwilling to risk another episode like that, he spent the remaining time working out. Alyx sparred with him, then Fenive and the others. The women warriors did well. They were as fast as he recalled, and amenable to the pointers he gave them on dodging and blocking his more powerful blows.

A few derkesthai watched them, from perches on rocks or sailing in silent circles overheard. They seemed entirely able to fly either with attention-getting claps of sound or with the stealth of apex predators. None of them approached the humans, and they only showed aggression when any of the humans accidentally moved past an invisible line around the cavern mouth. Then the humans were alerted with hissing, flapping wings, and occasional spouts of green flame.

As the afternoon light waned toward evening, the derkesthai's boundary began to expand. More of them ringed the apron of granite, gradually advancing, crowding the group toward the path—or the lethal pools, it became apparent. They would not be allowed to stay, as Oria had known.

Alyx cast an eye at the sun. "About an hour to sunset, Your Highness. Time to go."

Her warriors started saddling the horses again, putting their practice weapons away. Fenive retrieved Buttercup and saddled the warhorse for Lonen while he strained to see some movement, any hint of copper hair, in the depthless shadows of the cavern. None of them seemed surprised that Oria hadn't returned. He'd truly thought she might. In his mind, her voice taunted him for being a hopeless optimist, her eyes sparkling with merriment.

"Your Highness, you promised." Alyx and the others had mounted, ready to go. All save Fenive, who held out Buttercup's reins to him. Before he could protest, Alyx tipped her head at the encroaching ring of derkesthai. "And they seem inclined to enforce it."

Perhaps Oria had ordered them to drive him away. With an irrational spurt of anger, he wished he could give her a serious dressing down for her behavior. The anger died as quickly as it had arisen, quenched by the dread that he'd never see her again.

Saying nothing, he mounted Buttercup. Alyx and two of

her women started down the path, Fenive and the other two falling in behind him. It was the same pattern they'd taken on the ride in—one that made perfect sense for guarding an important personage on a narrow path—but he couldn't help feeling a bit like a prisoner being escorted to his doom.

As they rode through the stinking pools, blasts of heat rising from some, the ominous popping and crackling filling the air with forbidding sounds, the rest of his life seemed like the prison he imagined they took him to. Without Oria, the years ahead stretched as bleak as this landscape, as empty as his arms now felt. It seemed so strange to be riding without her in front of him. Where once her vibrant body had nestled, cold air found its way through openings in his cloak. No matter how he tried to close the gaps, the bitter cold crept in.

An omen of his future, no doubt.

He wanted to believe she'd arrive later that night, some-how finding her way to them, but even he couldn't imagine a situation where that would be possible. All day, as each hour dragged by, he'd known the likelihood of her return had diminished that much more. He knew her too well, and he'd understood what she hadn't said aloud.

The derkesthai would teach her to control the power in her, or they would nullify her. Lonen was only a Destrye warrior, a mind-dead barbarian, but he'd sensed it in her, the possibility of monstrosity. Only a few days earlier, he'd considered that he might someday have to kill his beloved, as Odymesen had killed his sorceress, to keep her from destroy-ing the world.

He dragged his thoughts away from that ugly scenario, deliberately summoning his optimism like taking up his iron battle-axe. Did Oria's magic feel this way to her when she strained to use it? Always he'd been able to find a bright side, to anticipate a positive outcome.

Painting the picture in his mind, he imagined Oria arriving at the cabin, maybe only a few hours behind them. The derkesthai escorted her there she'd say with a happy smile, and Chuffta on her shoulder would be bright-eyed and well. And she'd kiss Lonen again, repeating that startling press of her soft lips to his, that all-too-brief flash of contact, while he wrestled back his insane hunger for her and made himself thrust her away.

She's learned control, she would tell him, and now they can touch. All will be well. An idyllic happy ending.

Even without the idyll, she might arrive in the night, tired but fine. There, with him.

As much as he worked at it, though, he couldn't make himself believe it.

DERKESTHAI STREAMED AROUND her as she walked through the dimness, a milky river of an escort whose green eyes provided the only light, parting to allow her to pass, closing in before and behind. Not unlike Alyx's guarding of them. Only the derkesthai weren't protecting her so much as guiding her passage—and preventing her escape. She knew without any of them explaining that once she'd revealed herself to them, they wouldn't let her leave until she passed whatever test they had planned for her.

If she could've run back to Lonen, answered his tortured calling of her name, she might have. If she'd known how the derkesthai king would seize her mind, fillet and gut her thoughts and will like Chuffta devouring his prey, she might not have come here. Not even for Chuffta.

But she had. And with his warm weight cuddled against her body, she walked of her own free will—more or less— deeper into the endless cave. With no going back, she could only contemplate what she faced.

Ponen, they called her, as the Trom had. When that nightmare creature had spoken the word to her, it had sounded so foreign, impenetrable. Even her mother's explanation that the ancient word had once meant "potential" told her nothing. Princess Potential? Meaningless. Now it seemed she very nearly grasped its essence, as if some awakening dimension of herself already knew and she simply had to remember.

For better or worse, she would face the fire and emerge tempered—or perish in it.

Had Tania gone through this? That possessor of the mask and possession of Odymesen. Powerful, but ultimately damaged. Oria had caught the worry in Lonen's thoughts, followed it to the dread that she might become like Tania. However her ancestor had died, it had been tied to the mask and her magic. She hadn't looked deeper than that, as he'd buried whatever he knew, unwilling to contemplate it too closely. It was part and parcel of Lonen's resistance to her using the mask, which didn't matter unless she survived this.

She'd kept the mask in case she needed it after this, and it rode in its pouch dangling from her belt under the cloak. A garment she'd soon have to remove, as the longer she walked, the warmer the cavern became, dropping down toward the volcanic heat source deep inside. So many active minds all around, but remarkably restful for all that. Like Chuffta, the derkesthai seemed able to buffer themselves somehow, so their presence didn't penetrate her own thoughts and emotions.

She could probably live here in relative comfort, at least in that aspect, if they wouldn't let her leave. And if the derkesthai king consented not to kill her outright. Alive, yes, but she'd live out her life as a hollow shell of a person without Lonen. When she first met him, his masculine exuberance was like nothing she'd ever encountered. With his humor, sunny optimism, and sensual nature, he'd filled her up, nourishing an emptiness she hadn't known made her cold and hollow at the core. Marrying him had been like acquiring her own personal sun.

Without him, she'd be consigned to darkness.

Gradually the light changed. Instead of the black of the inside of a mountain, lit only by green eyeshine reflecting off white iridescent bodies, the warm shades of fire illuminated the passage. After a bit, she had to squint, the light nearly blinding, especially when she stepped into the vast dome.

She paused on the threshold, stilled by awe.

The cavern arched above her as high as the tallest towers of Bára and looked to be as far across as the vast Lake Scanda-malion. The floor sloped down, filled at the center by a lake, but this one of liquid fire. It glowed with a light too intense to look at for long. All around, the walls and ceiling of the dome glittered with reflected light, refracting and amplifying it. Peering at the wall beside her, she found it studded with crystal shards.

She'd seen a rock like this once. It had been a gift to the royal family of Bára—a round, dull and rough stone on the outside, but when broken open, it was hollow, the interior entirely lined with sharp, jagged crystals. This room was as if she stood inside that stone, only the crystals shone nearly diamond clear, rather than the purple of its smaller cousin.

Everywhere—flying, perched on outcroppings, nesting in

hollows—derkesthai thronged. She hadn't imagined so many of the rare creatures, even though the background chorus of mind-voices in her head had indicated their presence.

On a large, flat apron of rock by the lake, the king derkesthai reclined. For the first time, she got a good, long look at his immense size. Bigger than even the Trom dragons, but formed exactly the same as Chuffta, whose body she knew as well as her own, with none of the discolorations or distortions of the destructive dragons. Chuffta had insisted that he wasn't related to the Trom dragons, though she'd doubted his certainty even then. Her Familiar had also been young when they bonded on her seventh birthday. Her mother had always said they were of an age. Could Chuffta have left his colony so young that he didn't remember derkesthai of this size?

Though, as for that, none of the other derkesthai that she could see came close to the size of the king. Guardian Soldano, about four times Chuffta's size, came the closest—which was still as a boulder to a mountain.

"I am the only one like me," the king's mind-voice still thundered in her mind, though with each communication he'd reeled back the volume, as if learning her tolerance.

"How did you grow to such size, Great One?" she asked the question mentally. No need to voice it aloud as he wouldn't hear her across that vast space, and she was alone, without Lonen to listen in on her side of the conversation. She missed him already, with a vital ache, as if she'd left a part of herself behind.

"Can't you guess?" The dragon sounded drily amused—and somewhat impatient. *"Think, human child—what other creatures like me have you seen?"*

"The Trom dragons," she replied promptly, feeling much like a student sorceress in Bára again, answering the peremptory

questions of the high priestesses, that sense of being forever inadequate—and doubting her answers in the face of their disdain, when a moment before she'd been certain of them. *"But they're not white,"* she added, *"and not exactly the same as the derkesthai."*

"In much the same way the Trom are like you, but not exactly the same?"

Her legs felt suddenly weak, her head dizzy. The days of riding, short sleep—not to mention tearing her heart out and leaving it behind—and now this terrible interview… She longed to sit. But there was nowhere a human bottom could set itself without injury. Indeed, she saw no path to the relatively smooth cavern floor, only a jagged and uneven crystalline surface sloping down. Even if she could get to that floor, she might regret it, as it looked as hot as the ground they'd traveled past, where the snowflakes hissed into nothing on contact.

Interesting that they'd had a path suitable for horses and people to journey to this place at all, given how insular the colony acted otherwise. Clearly they didn't shun visitors entirely. They didn't exactly welcome them either.

"Well?" the king prompted.

Again, she'd regressed to her student days, when her mind wandered everywhere, landing on everything but what it should. *"The Trom seem far more different from me than the dragons do from you."*

"That's entirely a matter of perspective. Think again."

She didn't like to think about the Trom, with their elongated limbs and black eyes that swallowed their faces, devoid of mouths—or much in the way of human features at all. Like the masks the sorcerers and sorceresses of Bára wore. Like the one hanging from her belt.

The Trom had looked more like person-shaped spiders than human beings, as if their skin had been stretched over bone with everything else digested away. That image suddenly made her recall what Baeltya, the Destrye healer, had said when she diagnosed Oria as starving to death, how wraithlike and wan Oria had been. She'd gained weight since then and was much healthier, not nearly so skeletal, but the memory stirred unease in her. The Trom killed with a touch, and Oria's sorcerous abilities made her sensitive to touch—but not to the Trom. One had touched her, caressed her cheek like a lover, and she hadn't fallen down dead like everyone else the Trom touched, their bones jellied instantly.

Surely she wasn't like the Trom.

Chuffta weighed around her neck, making it ache. If only she could sit. *"Should Tukcha be healing Chuffta while we talk?"* she asked hopefully.

"No, because you are the one who is going to heal your Familiar. If you can. If you are able to absorb the lesson."

Oh no. Chuffta's life shouldn't ride on her being able to learn these things. All those years of failing to master the least child's magic trick rushed back at her. She couldn't do this.

Which meant she and Chuffta would both die here. She'd break her promise to return to Lonen. The Destrye would perish under Yar's aggression, and the people of Bára would suffer under the tyranny of their mad king. She had to try. Think it through, which meant facing ideas she dreaded.

"Are the Trom... former sorcerers, perhaps like my people, but changed over time by the magic they wield?"

"Yes."

All right then. She'd dreaded that answer, but knowing wasn't so terrible. Perhaps she could learn from their mistakes. *"What happened to them—why are they no longer human?"*

"Magic used incorrectly devours its wielder."

"What makes it incorrect?"

"You tell me."

She wanted to retort that if she knew, she wouldn't be facing this combination of examination and inquisition. *"I apologize, Great One. I am untutored. I left my home city shortly after receiving my mask and lack lessons in how to wield magic correctly."*

"Hmm. Promising. I might be able to work with you then."

That came as a welcome surprise—and gave her just enough hope not to despair. *"Why is that?"*

The great derkesthai sighed heavily, both a mental gust of exasperation and a physical one that blew dust across the stone he reclined on. **"Logic, child. Learn to employ it. If the Trom are former sorcerers, like those of your people, changed over time by the magic they wield, where did those sorcerers learn to wield the aforesaid magic?"**

"In the temples," she replied with dawning understanding, *"like the one at Bára."*

"Where you at least did not learn the wrong way to wield magic."

Excitement flared in her, burning away that dreadful enervation. *"What can you tell me about the correct way to wield magic then?"*

"You must have balance."

Hmm. *"The only balance I know is that of sgath and grien."*

"A good place to start. Like night and day, give and take, water and fire, Sgatha and Grienon. Think of these not as separate, but as a spectrum. If sgath and grien are the extremes, what is in the middle?"

"A balance of both." She whispered it aloud, her voice a surprise after the long silence.

"Indeed."

"So… if a human sorcerer is one extreme, is a Trom the other?"

"That could well be. And thus…?"

"Derkesthai to Trom dragon."

"Yes." His mind-voice, so much more tolerable now, hissed in satisfaction.

"And you… are the balance between?"

"I occupy a point of balance between extremes, yes."

"Are you telling me that a human sorcerer grew you to that size?" She remembered Chuffta's fascination with Tania's mask. How it made him want to be big.

"As a byproduct of other gifts."

"So you retain your derkesthai nature. You're not mindless like the Trom dragons."

"Like creates like."

She understood. *"That's why you want me to learn balance, so I won't become Trom."*

"Yes."

"Is it even possible?"

"We shall find out."

Wonderful. *"How long will this take?"*

He opened his man-sized green eyes even wider. **"Hopefully not longer than you can survive here."**

"Thank you—I appreciate that." She managed to convey that without excessive sarcasm.

"You do have a few things working in your favor. Nothing to unlearn, and your ancestress was able to learn this balance. Perhaps you will be like her."

"My ancestress… the sorceress who gave you your size was related to me?" Oria began to feel that she knew the answer. Ponen.

"The last Ponen before you. The last to have a derkesthai Familiar."

"My great-grandmother."

"Indeed. Now, let us talk about the nature of hwil and how

to guide the manifestation of your thoughts."

She mentally groaned. Back to this. She might as well be back in her tower at Bára. Only this time, Lonen waited for her. And Chuffta.

"Now, this might sting."

When he seized her thoughts and opened her mind, she screamed.

~ 13 ~

ORIA NEVER RETURNED.

Lonen lay awake all night, every scrape of a tree limb and crunching movement in the snow tricking his optimistic heart with the agonizing hope that it might be her.

It never was.

He told himself he was wakeful because he'd slept at midday, during that long nap to kill time while waiting outside of that cursed cavern. A lie, of course. But he lay there, wide awake, going back over the course of events, picking out all the decision points where he could have—*should* have—chosen a different path. He rehashed every conversation with Oria, coming up with better, more compelling arguments. With sick regret, he relived watching her walk into that yawning mouth without him.

He'd made so many mistakes, but nothing matched letting Oria go in there alone. He should've insisted on going with her. Hell, he should've tied her up and tossed her over Buttercup's back and not stopped until they reached Arill City. With a vicious, self-recriminating anger, he bitterly identified with his ancestors who'd kept their captive sorceresses close at hand. At least their women hadn't disappeared forever.

He lay there until the light shifted from black of night to pre-dawn dark, then forced himself to rise as the others did. If

Alyx and her soldiers hadn't been with him, he might've gone back to the cavern. Fuck his promises, his vows, his duty.

And fuck the throne.

Though Alyx said nothing, he felt the weight of her gaze, the burden of her expectation. She and her women supported his claim to the throne because of what he could do for them. Oria expected him to follow through because of what he needed to do for both their peoples.

So he'd go without argument. Even though none of it meant anything without Oria.

It should. Once upon a time, long ago, before he ever laid eyes on the copper-haired sorceress, he'd cared about nothing more than Dru and the Destrye. He'd planned to sacrifice himself any number of times for the cause of saving them. Though he'd never wanted the crown or his father's sword, he'd taken them up because it had fallen to him to do so. He'd easily accepted that his duty outweighed his desires.

His life had never been about what he wanted. He could do this just as he'd ridden into battle and as he'd taken the sword of kingship from his father's freshly dead hand. So he packed up and mounted Buttercup and rode hard for Arill City and the palace, ignoring how every fiber of him insisted they went in the wrong direction. They had until sunset the next day to make it back. Nolan would, no doubt, be watching the sun decline, waiting to pounce and seal Lonen's fate at the first possible moment.

He only wished he could face reclaiming the throne with wholehearted commitment. When had Oria become more important than anything else? With each league between him and his wife, he felt the distance strain the marriage bond. He'd become accustomed to it, that connection to her, where Oria burned like a bright spark in his soul. Now it dimmed, and he told himself the distance did it, not that her life force faded.

They rode too fast for conversation. Every hour saved now would allow everyone who supported him to breathe that much more easily. But that left him to the circle of his own thoughts, conversations from the night returning to play over and over.

"He thinks I enchanted you, enough that you'll abandon your duty to your people for me."

"Not because of magic. Out of love."

"It's the same in the end."

"It's not. Love is something good and pure, not some perversion of magic. If you'd enchanted me, it would be a kind of control, and you don't do that."

He didn't know what he thought anymore. Oria affected him on deep levels—ones he was more aware of than ever, as they throbbed with the pain of leaving her behind—but she'd never tried to control him. She'd given advice, sure. She'd insisted on following her own destiny, fighting with all the obstinacy in her nature, but she'd never controlled him.

Had she?

There'd been that moment when he'd felt the urge to go into the woods and leave Oria there with Buttercup, Chuffta, and the mask ensconced in the saddlebags. One moment he'd been ready to mount up again, the next urgently needing privacy. It had felt much like when the derkesthai king leaned on his will. In the aftermath of how that ill-advised encounter with the mask had harmed Oria, he hadn't thought about it.

Now it only mattered if he ever saw her again.

ORIA FELL TO her knees, sobbing and unable to withstand the pressure of the derkesthai king's mind.

"You're fighting me," he observed remorselessly, but thankfully also pulled back.

"I can't help it," she said aloud through her teeth, too exhausted to project with mind-voice alone, and the Great One seemed to be able to hear her regardless. Reflexively she cradled Chuffta in her arms, though the sling would prevent him from falling.

"You can help it," he replied. *"This is your mind. Who else controls it if not you?"*

Him, at the moment, though she didn't say that. "Some things are instinct. My heart is mine but I don't control whether it beats."

"Ah, but you could, if you trained to do it. Some sorcerers have."

"I bet it took all their lives to learn that," she replied bitterly. The sharp stones bit into her knees through the layers of skirts, and she dripped with sweat, though she'd long ago doffed the fur cloak and other outer layers. The derkesthai wouldn't care if she stripped naked, but the king hadn't let her pause long enough to do so. She'd love to take off the fur-lined stockings at least, but didn't dare remove her boots, lest she burn her feet or cut them to ribbons.

"It may have," the king mused. *"But what else is a life for?"*

"I don't have time for that," she gritted out.

"Everyone has the same amount of time, more or less. Granted, humans have shorter lives than derkesthai, but if you measure yourself against the sorcerers I mean, you are young yet."

"All right," she conceded. Arguing would waste even more time. She shifted to the least pointy spot she could find, hearing her skirts rip with weary resignation. At least the holes would vent some of the heat. She'd never thought, after leaving Bára's deserts, that she'd be too hot again. "Time presses on me because I need to heal Chuffta. I'm in this place with only the food and water I brought in, and I can't live long once that runs out. I've made promises to help Lonen. I can't spend years here."

"Human concerns."

"Well, yes. Because I'm human."

"Yes and no. You are no ordinary human. You aren't even an ordinary sorceress. You are Ponen. To realize your potential, you must rise above human concerns."

"I won't be doing much rising if I die from lack of water."

"There are many kinds of death. You cannot remain how you've been. To become a new version of yourself, the old you will have die."

Oh, that didn't sound ominous or anything. Since they seemed to be taking something of a break, she got out her flask and drank, salving her savage thirst. She also grabbed a handful of the nut, seed, and dried fruit mixture. "Metaphorical death is not the same as physical death," she pointed out.

"I see in your mind a woman telling you that she'd seen people in better condition than you who'd starved to death."

He drew that scene forward in her mind, a strange sensation that she tried to accept without resistance. "Yes, the healer Baeltya treated me—and arranged for me to have better food, the kind my body was used to."

"But why didn't you die?"

"Because I got the right food in time."

"Incorrect. Look with my eyes."

An even more odd sensation, skewing her internal vision to see her own memories as the derkesthai king saw them, like looking at a reflection of herself in a mirror, reflected by another mirror behind that. Through his eyes she perceived different colors, reminding her of seeing through Chuffta's eyes, only magnified greatly.

"Your Familiar will also refine his senses over time. Concentrate. What do you see?"

Strings of energy flowing in and around her, and layers of glowing light, of shades no human eye could perceive. "Is that how magic looks to you?"

"Yes. And how it could look to you, if you will only open your eyes."

She sighed. Always back to this. "If I knew how, I would." She took a judicious sip of water. Already more than half empty. She had no way of knowing how much time had passed, if it might be still daylight. If Lonen had left.

Who was she kidding? It had been ages. They'd all left.

"Let me open them for you," the king suggested, not for the first time.

Lowering her physical lids, she nodded, letting him push around in her thoughts without resisting. Much. It felt like allowing someone to dig around in her gut while she nodded and smiled, only not painful—just impossible to do without flinching. This time the exhaustion worked in her favor. Each time he invaded her mind, she had less strength.

Vaguely it occurred to her that this might be incredibly foolish. She had no reason to trust this dragon, to believe any of his claims. What if he worked with the Trom and this was part of a scheme to destroy her? With an involuntary mental kick, she thrust the derkesthai king out of her mind.

"Ouch!" he scolded. *"If you don't trust me, why are we even bothering with this?"*

"I apologize, Great One," she said, weariness substituting for humility. "It's a reflex."

"You are strong," he replied grudgingly. *"Perhaps too strong."*

"Too strong for what?"

"If you cannot let go of your fears and paranoia, then you will become like the Trom. I cannot save you. Or your Familiar."

Despite the stab of fear they incited, those words gave her an insight, something she likely should've realized earlier, but hadn't, as if a light had illuminated a room. "The Trom seek power to be strong. So they can't be harmed."

"Yes, the human animal drive to kill or be killed. You must rise above that, want something more."

"Wanting to live tops most everything else," she pointed out, adjusting Chuffta, who slept as ever.

"You could have lived and not come here. Why are you here? Why haven't you left?"

"I couldn't just let Chuffta die."

"Exactly. This is the only reason I've agreed to help you. If you had come here for any other reason, I would have simply had you put down."

"You're not helping because Chuffta is one of you, but because I'm doing this out of love, not for power."

"There. Concentrate on the love. Give up protecting yourself, your human concerns."

She didn't have to trust, or even not flinch. She need only think about Chuffta, and how she loved him. How she loved Lonen, a different love, equally as powerful and selfless. And beyond that, a larger circle of love, for family, for the people who'd been kind to her, for the Destrye and Bárans, the deserts and forests crying for water, and even for the moons that waxed and waned, pushing and pulling.

It didn't matter if it hurt, or if it killed her—because all them were worth her sacrifice.

"Ah," the derkesthai king said in satisfaction, and *pulled.*

Oria shattered, her mind splintered, and her body fell like the victims of the Trom had, crumpling into piles of boneless goo. Her flask rolled away, clattering as it tumbled down the rocks.

LONEN FELT A slicing, deep inside, like a knife cutting something a blade should never touch. He gasped aloud, and Buttercup, exquisitely sensitive to his rider's signals, wheeled in place and ran at top speed in the opposite direction. The bite inside him eased and Lonen found himself smiling, ever so relieved to be going back for Oria.

This was right. At last he was going in the correct direction.

If they hadn't been riding so long and hard, if Buttercup hadn't been so recently injured and healed, if the forest path weren't so narrow and twisting, Alyx on her inferior steed would never have been able to catch up with them. He could've ignored her cries, her calls for him to halt, to wait, but when she crowded them on a tight curve, he couldn't allow Buttercup to crush them into a tree with his bulk.

Biting back his frustration, he pulled Buttercup up and Alyx—the warrior woman taking impressive initiative—pushed her horse past them and turned the mare to squarely block the path. The others thundered up behind them, fencing him in. No concerns there. That wasn't the direction he intended to go.

"Your Highness," she panted, out of breath from yelling

during the breakneck chase. "How may I assist?"

"By getting out of my way," he replied, only snarling a little at having to state the obvious. Buttercup took a step forward, but Alyx's mare held firm, obeying though her nostrils quivered in agitation.

"Your Highness, we cannot afford to backtrack at all or we won't make it to Arill City in time."

"That's fine. Let Nolan have the throne. He was meant to be king anyway. I won't fight him for it."

Several of the women murmured to each other behind him, and Alyx flicked a glance at them and then to him. The raw betrayal in her eyes might've gutted him, if feeling Oria's pain hadn't done that already. "If you'd treated Prince Nolan as he's treated you, Your Highness, he'd have been officially declared dead when he disappeared on the battlefield. Would you have challenged him for the throne, were your positions reversed?"

"Of course not." He nudged Buttercup another step, closing enough to see the strain in Alyx's throat as she defied him. She didn't give way, however, full of the resolve in her cause that he lacked. Abruptly weariness flooded him. He was so tired of fighting—the Bárans, the golems, his own brother— and of the doubts about Oria, the sun of his life. Oria loved him for himself. If he went to her and said he'd given up being king and wanted only to be a man, with her, she'd still love him.

But she'd be disappointed. She'd look at him with that same expression as Alyx, the sour taste of his failure to measure up in her eyes. Inside him, the knife turned, Oria's pain throbbing like a living wound. "Oria..." he said, only realizing he said her name aloud when he heard the broken sound.

Alyx's face crumpled with compassion, though she didn't yield. "Her Highness is a strong woman. As strong—or stronger—as any I've met. She wouldn't thank you for turning your back on your mutual cause, on both your peoples, by coming back for her."

She'd overheard a great deal, which should be no surprise. He gave one last look at the path beyond Alyx, knowing he could take it if he chose, then closed his heart to it. "You're right," he told her. "I apologize."

"Take a fast break while we're stopped," Alyx called to the others. "We'll continue to Arill City shortly." She lowered her voice again, shaking her head. "Don't apologize, Your Highness. You have a great heart, which will make you a great king. When there's love like you and Her Highness have, it's difficult to put duty over it. That you will speaks more highly of you than anything."

"With the occasional pointed reminder," he replied wryly, fishing water out of the bags, trying not to think about whether Oria had enough, whether she'd even survive.

"I'm happy to serve as your conscience, Your Highness." Alyx handed him some jerky. "I'm aware my investment is self-serving. I want you as my king, and I'm willing to be ruthless to make sure of it. Though I'm sorry to see you suffer her absence."

"You don't think I'm enchanted?" he asked, before he meant to. Emotional exhaustion getting to him, to ask her such a thing. Though… who else could he ask? Everyone had an opinion about Oria. Alyx seemed to be one of the few who didn't loathe the sorceress on principle.

Alyx chewed her jerky thoughtfully, giving the question such due consideration—and with no surprise that he'd asked—that he knew she'd heard discussions of the possibility.

She swallowed, shaking her head decisively. "I don't know much about enchantment, but it seems to me that if the sorceress had magicked you, Your Highness, you'd be a lot happier. Only love, hopeless and impossible, makes anyone this miserable."

"That's… unusual logic."

She shrugged. "Seems to me, Your Highness, that if you wanted an easy way of it, you wouldn't have married a Báran sorceress. You wouldn't be determined to marry her again under Arill's hand either. I've seen how she looks at you—she'd give you the last drop of blood in her body if you asked, whether you made her Queen of Dru or not. I don't know, but if *I* had the kind of power she does, I'd be making you dance a merry tune, not sending you away."

It made sense. So much that he wondered how he'd let himself get confused. "Once I claim the throne, if Oria hasn't returned, I'm coming back for her."

Alyx nodded as if she expected as much. "We'll come with you."

Neither of them mentioned the possibility that there would be nothing left of her to retrieve.

IN THE BEGINNING, there was only the formless void, containing everything and nothing, only potential, nothing yet realized.

The old temple words rolled through Oria's mind, comforting as those early childhood sayings can be. Like nursery songs and the feeling of being loved. Odd to feel that sense of safety as she wandered the void. Formless in a place of nothingness. Alone and yet not lonely.

"Because I'm here with you. I promised I'd always be with you."

She looked, but had no eyes. No ears, either. Still, the voice resonated in her being, requiring no physical senses. Emotion existed in this void, because hope, impossibly keen-edged, stabbed at her. *"Chuffta?"*

"Of course. Who else?"

"You're alive!"

He tutted at her. *"You knew that."*

"Yes and no. Your body..." Memory returned in vivid clarity. *"Are you alive?"*

"The part of me that is eternal is here with you, yes, silly."

Oh no. That didn't sound good. She'd died. She failed that final lesson and her body had died, along with Chuffta's. They were together in the afterlife, which wasn't at all the solace it should've been.

"Not yet, but we will be soon if you don't act. I'm a young derkesthai. I'd like my body back, please."

As did she. *"I don't know what to do."*

He shrugged. *"You're the sorceress. You are Ponen. Take the potential and make form from the void."*

"Oh, is that all?"

"Yes." He mentally flicked his tail.

"But how?"

"Magic," he replied, with crisp certainty, as if the answer had been obvious all along. *"You have all the tools within you, the ability and the knowledge. Use it. And when you give me a body again, make it a* big *one."*

No, it wasn't enough to use it. She remembered now. She must use it with balance, and out of love. What had the Destrye said about their goddess? Arill made the world from the void out of love and loneliness. She manifested reality to share the delight of being.

Oria tried to be like that, like a pure and perfect goddess, full of love for all creation. She reached for her sgath…

"Not like that," the derkesthai king inserted into her mind. *"Not the way you did before. You've shed your former body, now let go of the old you."*

She tried, letting it all fall away. A kind of saying goodbye.

"Now: touch the magic. Take it into yourself. Without reservation or defense."

Touch it? Let it flood her? She'd lived her whole life not touching or being touched, living atop her isolated tower, protected from exactly this. Alive but not living. So afraid of dying that she'd walled out all of life.

Of course that had to change, so that she could. She opened her portals, ruthlessly dropping all caution and reserve.

"Be careful, Oria," Chuffta warned. *"Don't—"*

Too late. The wave crashed over her, severing her from everything.

~ 14 ~

L ONEN FELT IT the moment Oria died.

The bright, warm spark of her inside him simply flickered out. Gone as if it had never been. Leaving him cold and empty. As much as her pain and torment had tugged at him, as much as he'd hated the gradual attenuation of their marriage bond as he rode farther and farther away from her—this sudden loss was so much worse.

He must have made a sound. A startled cry like a man wounded in ambush, because the two nearest riders ahead of him spun their horses, weapons drawn. The two behind rode up to flank him with their weapons facing out.

"Your Highness!" said Fenive. "Are you hurt?"

Alyx was there in moment, but he was already shaking his head. "I'm fine. Keep riding." No reason to hesitate now.

"Your Highness?" Alyx questioned.

"She's gone," he replied shortly.

They all fell silent, somber with shock, perhaps shared grief.

"You're certain."

"We were magically married. I've been attached to her since that moment. No longer."

As one, the women made the sign of Arill, bowing their heads in prayer. With the forest canopy arching overhead, the early winter evening descending—and the near moon, Sgatha, hanging full, round, and rosy in the sky between the stark branches—the woods felt like a temple. The murmurs of them speaking the prayer for the dead only reinforced the strangely sanctified moment.

Lonen couldn't bring himself to speak the words, or truly even listen. He'd been alone back on that plain before the walls of Bára, and he was alone again. Except for cold duty.

And retribution.

If Nolan hadn't driven them away, Oria and Chuffta would've stayed safe in the palace. Lonen might have only his duty to his people—and Oria's—but that was something. He'd cling to that. And he would make Nolan pay.

The last whispers of the prayer faded away, taken up by the susurrus of a wind high in the bare branches.

"Let's ride," he growled.

This time, he took point. Let the others keep up if they could.

Darkness swirled around them, formless and without sign of light. Sgatha had fallen out of sight behind the mountains, and even Grienon on his wild and impetuous path had disappeared over the horizon. In the very early dawn, no habitations had lit lanterns yet.

After riding at a breakneck pace all night, they'd been forced to slow. The horses still sensed the trail, through scent or some sensitivity of their hooves, but the riders had to be wary of unseen dangers.

Besides, not all the horses in their group possessed Buttercup's stalwart endurance. Lonen would've left them behind, if Alyx's warriors hadn't been so determined to keep up—pushing themselves and their mounts to do it. A great deal to prove, he supposed, and because he knew they'd kill themselves trying rather than risk being inadequate, he restrained his snapping impatience.

Finally he agreed to stop for a short break. They'd reached the outlying farmlands around Arill City, the ones scored by the Trom dragons. They knew it because the muffled and crowding shadows of trees had opened up to the echoing space of a flat landscape. And a glimmer of light showed finally, the snow-covered fields picking up the glow from beyond the horizon. In another hour or so the sun would rise, and they'd have all the day to reach Arill's Temple and declare Lonen alive and ready to face Nolan's challenge.

Something truly dire would have to happen now to prevent that. As the worst thing possible had already occurred, Lonen couldn't imagine what could stop him now. He'd fight Nolan, probably kill his brother to exact revenge for Oria's death, and afterward there would be time to mourn.

Besides, Nolan might insist on having the duel right then and there—and Lonen would welcome the opportunity to vent his rage and grief on the prideful sod who'd caused all this sorrow. It would be best if he arrived rested and ready to fight.

So he agreed to Alyx's proposal that they rest in an abandoned farmhouse, one that had escaped the fires and destruction. They gave the horses food and water, ate the last of their own food, and tried to sleep a little.

Some of the women did sleep, with that enviable ability to grab rest at any time. Lonen had once possessed it, but he'd long since passed into an attenuated state of hypervigilance.

He'd sleep when he was king. Arill knew he'd never take another queen. His bed would remain empty and Lonen would devote all of himself to his duty.

The image of himself, a mad king in his own right, prowling the palace at Dru in his loneliness, made him too restless to even try for sleep. Instead he joined Alyx on the porch of the farmhouse where she perched on the rail, cupping a mug of hot broth, staring out over the fields. The morning light revealed the burnt landscape with stark brutality.

"I hadn't seen it," she said. "We heard about the Trom attack, of course, and I thought I understood how bad it was. But I hadn't seen it for myself yet."

He leaned against the rail, the frozen landscape much the same as his heart, the scorched earth showing in ridges of scars against the ice-encrusted snowdrifts. Lonen wasn't a farmer, though since he'd become king he'd learned more than he'd ever cared to know about what the land required to bear crops. Looking at the baked earth, so slick it wouldn't even hold snow cover, he wondered how the Destrye could possibly recover these fields. They might have to abandon Dru after all.

The prospect didn't bother him as much as it once had. At least then he'd be far from anything that reminded him of Oria.

"I keep thinking," Alyx continued into his silence, "that if we'd been there, if so many of us hadn't retreated to the hermitage with the queen, we might've been able to help or maybe—"

"Don't," he cut her off. "No one could've done anything. The Trom dragons are unstoppable. We can no more fight them than we can thwart lightning or make it rain."

"I can see that now," she replied after a pause, "what destruction they wreak."

He didn't say anything. There was nothing to say.

"How will we fight them, then?" she finally asked. "I have no doubt that you'll defeat Nolan and claim the throne, but what do we do then? I mean, may I ask what your plan is, Your Highness?" The hastily added addendum to her plaintive question made him smile, though bitterly, because he had no answer.

"My plan was Oria," he confessed. "She could've fought the Trom with her sorcery. We'd thought to drive away their dragons and supplant her brother Yar, so that these monsters couldn't be brought against us again. Without her..."

"Ah." With that breathed sound, more of a sigh than an actual word, Alyx acknowledged the powerful inevitability of their doom.

"I think we'll have to leave," he said. "Take the Destrye and go as far as we can."

"We will of course go wherever you lead, Your Highness."

"Will my mother, do you think?"

Alyx hesitated too long, perhaps searching for a soothingly noncommittal answer. Lonen chuckled mirthlessly. "Never mind. I know she won't."

"There will be others, Your Highness, who won't leave. You know that. The ones who've lived here their entire lives, the ones who know they'd die on the journey and would rather lay their bones in Dru, the stubborn, the ones so hopelessly optimistic they'll cling to the hope of victory long after everything points to defeat."

Hopelessly optimistic. How many times had Oria accused him of just that? Countless times. She'd said that nothing could defeat his sunny outlook. Grief surged bitter as the tides of Bára as he—more than anything in the world—longed to tell Oria that she was wrong, something *could* kill his native optimism. All it had taken was her death.

"I won't force anyone to leave," he decided. "Anyone who wants to stay and fight it out can." Maybe he'd stay with them. That would at least end his misery in a noble and fitting way. The king perishing with his kingdom.

"But you will lead the people," Alyx insisted.

"Yes," he conceded. He could hardly defeat Nolan and then refuse to lead as a king should. And there was no question of whether he'd fight Nolan. His brother would pay. "Speaking of which, rouse your warriors. Let's be done with this."

"Yes, Your—" Her words choked off as an arrow pierced her shoulder and pinned her to the porch post.

Lonen ducked before he fully processed what had happened, his iron axe in hand. Even in sleep he kept it near—and it was not lost on him at the moment how fully useless it was against an enemy armed with bows and arrows. Alyx gasped, tugging at the arrow, and another thudded into her, making her cry out. The warrior women shouted from within, and the farmhouse door flew open.

"Stay down!" He yelled. "Fenive, get to an upper window with your bow." He levered up next to Alyx, hating himself for using her as cover as he peered past her hip—but also ignoring her pleas to leave her and save himself.

Bows and arrows meant people, not golems or sorcerers. Another arrow flew past him, narrowly missing his head and hitting the wall behind him. A volley of arrows shot outward from the upper story, toward a low hedge by the road. Using the cover, he scrambled back, breaking off the arrow as he rolled inside.

Destrye arrows, the sort used by the palace guard. Fury boiled up in him, like fire that might erupt from his throat. No longer caring about his safety—a ridiculous concept—he charged out the door, shouting, "Nolan, you fucking coward!

Show yourself."

No arrows thudded into him. Silence, except for Alyx's ragged, pained breathing, fell heavy in the crisp winter air. "Hold your fire," a man called, and stepped out into the open, followed by five more.

Twenty more emerged from the copse of trees across the road. And forty more from around the side of the house. All heavily armed, and wearing the uniform of the palace guard.

Lonen and his six warriors couldn't possibly prevail. "This is treachery," he ground out. "You betray your king."

The leader sketched a bow, a reasonably respectful one, given the circumstances. "With apologies, Prince Lonen, we serve His Highness King Nolan. Given your wartime desertion of the Destrye forces, His Highness has taken up the sword and wreath of Dru. He sent us to escort you back home, should you appear."

Lonen bit out a harsh, disbelieving laugh at the insulting words. "An escort? Is that what you call it when you shoot at loyal soldiers in the king's party?"

"We saw only a woman and figured her for one of the prince's camp followers," the man replied. "Lay down your weapons, turn over the sorceress to us, and we'll escort you home peaceably, Prince Lonen."

So that was the way of it. No sense in lying about Oria's fate, however, and better to remove that chip from the bargaining table. "The sorceress Oria is dead," he informed them, tossing his useless battle-axe aside. "I'm going to tend to Captain Alyx. We won't fight you."

Turning his back on them in deliberate dismissal, he checked Alyx's wounds. Mostly attention-getting and not piercing any vital organs, the wounds nevertheless bled enough to kill her if they delayed treatment. "Thanks for the promotion," she said, her lips stretching across clenched teeth in a pretense of a grin. "But don't worry about me."

"We're getting you to a healer, Captain," he replied. "I'm breaking off the arrows. On my mark." She screamed at the first, passed out on the second. He'd have expected the same of any man, so hopefully she wouldn't see it as a weakness. Not an easy burden to labor under, having something to prove. Camp follower, his ass. Fenive arrived just in time to help him slide Alyx's unconscious body off the shortened stakes pinning her to the post, so she took over staunching the bleeding.

Lonen turned to face Nolan's men, who'd assembled in the farmhouse's erstwhile yard. Scanning the faces, he identified several men he knew well—though at least none from his own battalion, which provided obscure comfort—and a number who looked familiar. "So Nolan is too much of a coward to face me in a legitimate duel," he noted.

The leader—who Lonen didn't know at all, which meant he'd likely been one of Nolan's men, probably had traveled with him through the tunnels from the underground lake at Bára—reddened in impotent anger. No doubt they were under orders not to kill Lonen outright. A coup would look bad, whereas compelling Lonen's submission would work entirely in Nolan's favor. A number of the other men, however, shuffled uneasily and wouldn't meet his eyes. This wasn't how the Destrye fought, not though guile and treachery.

"If you wish to challenge His Highness King Nolan to a duel for the throne, you may seek Arill's blessing for it," the leader replied stiffly.

"I'll take it up with the goddess," Lonen answered. "However, since *Prince* Nolan challenged me, and I have been ruling as rightful king since the deaths of my father and Prince Ion, I believe the question of a duel has been resolved."

The leader shook his head. "I'm sorry, Prince Lonen, but you abdicated when you abandoned the throne and crown."

"Don't be ridiculous, Mott," Fenive snapped. "You can't declare His Highness dead until sundown tonight. The seven days aren't up yet."

Mott smiled thinly. "Indeed that's true, but Prince Lonen would have to present himself at Arill's Temple before then."

"So? We're a couple of hours' ride away at best, and it's only just after sunrise," Fenive argued.

The plot dawned on Lonen, and he cursed himself for being so thick and slow. The profound betrayal gutted him—another ambush, one so foul he'd never imagined it possible. "You don't mean to escort us to Arill City, Mott, is it?"

"You don't remember me, do you, Prince Lonen? No, the likes of me wasn't good enough for you and your battalion. But His Highness recognizes worth—and rewards loyalty. It was my honor to volunteer to escort you to Arill's Temple, and I will. Eventually. Well after the sunset deadline. I suggest you make yourselves comfortable. Tomorrow morning should be soon enough to leave."

Fenive made an incoherent sound of anger, but Lonen gestured her to silence. "Captain Alyx will die before tomorrow morning without healing."

Mott gave Alyx's prone body a cursory and contemptuous glance. "Alyx—and you, Fenive—have always offended Arill's eye with your aspirations to men's work. If the goddess chooses to strike you down for your blasphemy, then so be it."

"I believe it was your archer who struck her down, not Arill," Lonen replied mildly.

Mott flushed, hand clenching his sword as if he'd love to use it on them. "Don't you defile the name of the goddess!" he shouted.

"I am still your prince," Lonen answered, striding down the steps and meeting the point of Mott's sword. "Though you may have been misled over who rules Dru and the Destrye, you *will* give me the respect of rank."

Mott's lip curled. "You won't have to be ritually declared dead if you are truly dead."

Several of Mott's men made sounds of agreement—but more seemed dismayed, shifting uneasily. "Will you kill me then?" Lonen asked softly, leaning his chest into the point of the sword. He'd almost welcome the slicing pain, cleaving his broken heart in actuality as well as metaphorically, followed by the sweet release of death.

"His Highness is right," Mott breathed. "You *are* insane, driven mad by that foul, foreign sorceress who—"

Lonen's hand shot out, seizing Mott by the throat, taking him so by surprise that the sword skidded off Lonen's leather breastplate, carving only a shallow cut. Lonen had suffered far worse and for sorrier reasons. "You don't speak of her," he said, spacing out the words, as Mott was clearly a numbskull. "Am I insane because death doesn't frighten me, that I'd be just as pleased to squash you like the bug you are and lose the throne to my power-mad brother—or because Oria enchanted me to want the throne above all? Both can't be true."

Mott gasped like a fish out of water, unable to breathe, much less answer, and Lonen took a savage satisfaction in it, vising his grip. But the image of the fish reminded him of that day at Lake Scandamalion, when Chuffta landed the stardew fish and Oria scolded him for it. How full of love he'd been— and terror that he'd lose her to the seductive power of the mask. Now he'd lost her entirely and he longed to go back to that moment, to turn time to prevent the cascade of events.

"Prince Lonen, sir, release the captain. Please." Several

swords pointed at him, ringing him round with lethal edges. One sharp blade lay against the arm holding Mott immobile, the face above the sword a familiar one. "Please, Your Highness," the man urged, expression contorted with fear and dread. "Don't make us do this."

With a surprising amount of effort, Lonen forced his fingers to open, and Mott fell to a crumpled pile at his feet. Two men moved forward to drag him away. Lonen met the gaze of the man who'd spoken. "Nestor. I wouldn't have expected this of you."

Nestor met his gaze, firming his chin, though guilt crawled over his face. "It hasn't been an easy week, Your Highness. We are simple men. Our loyalty and fealty should be simple also, not a question of choice. We're doing our best to keep the peace."

Lonen supposed he could understand that. Their rightful king had disappeared, slipped out like a thief in the night, with no explanation. Because no explanation was possible. "How are things in Arill City?" he asked.

"Uncomfortable, Your Highness, though guards such as we are not privy to much of what transpires."

Hmm. That meant a lot of political wrangling behind closed doors. And conducted quietly enough that not even servants' gossip carried it to the men at arms. "Did Queen Vycayla and her retinue arrive?"

Nestor glanced from side to side, though who he feared overhearing such a straightforward answer—one that should be common knowledge—wasn't clear. "Yes, Your Highness. Two days ago."

He said nothing more, and Lonen didn't press. Whatever transpired within the royal family was beyond these men. "If you prevent me and my party from reaching Arill's Temple before sundown, you'll be thwarting Arill's divine right to determine who will be King of the Destrye—and jeopardizing Captain Alyx's life."

Nestor, sweat rolling down his temple, swallowed hard. But his sword didn't waver. "Begging your pardon, Your Highness, but you'll have to sort that out with the goddess and King Nolan. We don't dare disobey."

"You'll betray me but not my brother, is that it?" Lonen asked mildly, though he boiled with defeated rage. To come this close and fail… He should've gone back for Oria. Would she still have died if he'd kept going when he tried to turn back? The possibility throbbed with such tender agony that he had to set it aside.

"Your Highness, I—ah, I…" Nestor stammered as he groped for an answer, so Lonen waved him silent.

"Would you at least detail some men to carry Captain Alyx to the temple, so she won't die?" he asked instead.

Nestor swallowed again, still bravely meeting Lonen's gaze though panic lit his eyes. "Our orders are to let none of you past this point. Not until after sunset."

Lonen stared him down another long, endless moment, then called to Fenive. "Take Captain Alyx inside and do your best to tend to her. We might as well stay warm while we wait out this treacherous imprisonment."

He turned his back on the sweating Nestor and climbed the steps to help carry Alyx indoors, glancing back at the sound of boots on the wooden steps. Nestor starting to follow. "Not you or your men, Nestor. You can hold your vigil outdoors."

Nestor bowed, out of habit, stopping himself halfway at an uncertain angle. "And Captain Mott? Sir?"

Lonen didn't bother to look at the man gasping in the snow. "Let him rot for all I care."

~ **15** ~

NEVER HAD A day passed so slowly. As if to mock him, the sun broke through the clouds that had hung over their journey, shining with malicious glee as it glided across the arc of the sky. With each hour that passed, as it became more and more undeniable that he'd lost everything—sacrificed what he loved most to gain nothing at all—Lonen sank further into gloom.

Alyx still lived, but barely. They could do nothing more for her, having stopped the bleeding and closed her wounds. Her ragged panting filled the cabin's silence. Lonen stared into the fire, adding the decision to allow Alyx and her warriors to accompany them to the long list of bad choices, another in the cascade that it seemed he should be able to stop, if only he could go back in time.

A ridiculous exercise, crawling over every detail and choosing the exact spot he'd jump back to in order to change the course of their lives. Selfishly, he wouldn't want to change meeting and marrying Oria, so finding the point where they still found each other, but didn't reach this point of utter failure, was tricky.

Not that he *could* turn back time, but the riddle gave him something to do. By turns despondent and burning with the furious need to act, plotting how he'd change all of this, he prodded his pain over and over. That and plotting his revenge against Nolan at least kept him occupied.

At one point, Fenive sat beside him. "If we found a way to sneak out, perhaps through the back, we could—"

"They outnumber us by too much," he cut her off, unable to listen to the hope in her voice. No wonder his optimism had annoyed Oria so. "They have the numbers to encircle the house entirely. Any escape attempt would get you all killed and leave me stuck in the same spot."

"You can't just give up!" She sounded aghast, belatedly adding, "Your Highness."

"I'm not giving up. I'm acknowledging defeat. Nolan outmaneuvered me. The game is done—we're stalemated and just waiting for the final piece to fall."

"But Your Highness, we could—"

"No, Fenive. Just no. I'm not getting one more person killed in my bid to hold a throne I never wanted in the first place. Nolan will be a good enough king." Until Lonen killed him, opening the way for their youngest brother Amon. He'd be a good king—he'd have to be, as the Destrye would be fresh out of Archimago's sons.

"Not good for us," she replied bitterly.

"Then you're no worse off than you were a week ago," he replied. He wished he could say as much for himself.

"That's not true," Fenive shot back. "A week ago I didn't know to hope for more. Now I do and I grieve the loss of that."

"Hope is a terrible tease," he agreed, and she gave him an odd look. "It's better for us to resign ourselves to the grind of fate and hope to hell that Arill has some plan in all this wreckage and disaster."

"Maybe the goddess will provide a miracle yet," Fenive

offered.

"That's what it would take: a miracle. I wouldn't advise holding your breath."

Fenive didn't say more—he'd apparently been crushing enough to silence even her youthful enthusiasm. Once he'd believed that Arill had guided him to Oria, that the goddess had led him to marry and love the difficult and powerful sorceress, that She had intended for him to be king and lead the Destrye—and perhaps the Bárans, too—to a peaceful prosperity. He and Oria could have united their people and lived out long lives breeding children born of both races to coax the world back into balance.

But it had all been foolish dreams and wishful thinking. Sparks from the campfire, burning bright as they whirled in their mad dance, then vanishing to ash.

In the morning, once Nestor—or Mott, should he be sadly recovered—Lonen wouldn't return to Arill City. He and Buttercup would go back to the derkesthai colony and recover Oria's body. He'd at least give her a proper burial, and hold vigil over her ashes for the full twelve days, as befitted a true queen.

After that... he would make his plans, and strike Nolan down. He hadn't decided when or how. A future beyond the following morning seemed both infinite and nonexistent. But he felt better deciding that much—that he and Buttercup, riding into the mountain winter. Maybe they wouldn't come back. *Some commit suicide that way—going off into the winter. They say that once you get cold enough, you start to feel warm and sleepy. You fall asleep and never wake up again.* He remembered telling Oria that by the lake, her magical copper eyes bright with interest in her pale face, bloodless from the chill.

Eyes he'd never again look into.

Shouts outside roused him from the depthless funk. Something had the men stirred up. He couldn't bring himself to care.

"Your Highness!" Fenive said from the window, her voice urgent. "You have to see this."

"No, I really don't," he answered. Even standing up seemed beyond him.

"But, the men…" she trailed off, as screaming from outside overtook her words. The roar of flame followed, the unmistakable sound of tornadic fire. "It's a dragon. A real *dragon*."

The Trom had returned already? A small, petty, and vicious part of him celebrated. There—let Nolan explain *that* away. Let his brother fight the implacable enemy he hadn't believed in. That would be a fair portion from Arill's hand.

But cold duty, his final and unfeeling companion, prodded him to his feet. The Destrye were his people still and always. Even these misguided soldiers holding them hostage only followed the orders of the man who'd declared himself their king. They didn't deserve to die at the hands of the Trom.

Not that Lonen could do anything to save them. He'd tried, and failed.

Surprisingly stiff from sitting still so long, after pushing his body so hard the last few days—and from letting the heaviness of despair settle into his bones, no doubt—he made his way like an old man to the window, bracing himself for the sight of the Trom dragons darkening the sky and setting fire to everything beneath.

Instead, he blinked, the bright sun on the vast whiteness of snow dazzling his vision. Squinting, he tried to refocus, because surely that couldn't be….

"It's Oria!" Fenive clutched his arm, jumping in her excitement. "On a white dragon!"

He couldn't reply, because his breath had guttered out when his heart stopped beating.

It was Oria.

It had to be her, with that distinctive and brilliant shine of copper hair, snapping in the wind like a banner as her iridescent white dragon steed dove, driving the men screaming before it. Bright green flame ripped out, melting the snow in broad streaks.

Men hurtled themselves in all directions, scattering like sparrows before a stooping hawk, leaving their weapons behind in their terror. Lonen ripped open the front door, ran down the front steps, and waved his arms in the air. "Oria!" Her name shredded his lungs, the cold air following hard to choke him. Overcome, he fell to his knees, the snow burning chill through his pants as it soaked in. The white dragon wheeled, spinning midair, then backwinged.

"Oria." He struggled to his feet as the dragon landed, watching him with dancing green eyes that seemed so familiar, though so very large. It bent down, allowing Oria—still clad in her red gown and shadowcat fur cloak, though the gown looked burnt in places, and torn—to slide off his back. She stumbled a little at the impact, but recovered and ran toward him, hair brighter than the sun.

"Lonen!" she hurled herself at him, hitting him like an arrow of intoxicating woman. He wrapped his arms around her, laying his cheek against her silken hair, breathing in her scent—an odd combination of sulfurous fumes, derkesthai musk, and her sweet self—and absorbing her heat. It wasn't possible. Very likely he'd fallen into a delirium born of grief and heartbreak, but at least Arill had given him this gift, this last moment of holding his wife.

"Oria," he muttered, ragged, and like a prayer. She leaned

back and framed his face with her bare hands, her touch like the hand of the goddess, sparking through his bloodstream. Her copper eyes, wide and flecked with gold, streamed with tears. She gave him a smile somehow both radiant and tremulous.

"Oh, Lonen. I thought I might never see you again." Burying her fingers in his hair, she dragged his head down as she raised herself up on tiptoe, sealing her lips to his.

He groaned at the unbearably enticing sweetness of her mouth, the incredibly soft give of her lips and the fierce demand as she kissed him, drinking him in and giving back at once. She nearly vibrated in his arms, a tiny sun exploding with magic and sexuality.

From this he understood that none of it was real.

It couldn't be, as Oria couldn't kiss him like this. Never had he felt the sensual slide of her tongue, the piercingly intense sensation of her dewy soft skin under his hands. He must be dying or losing his mind, but if it brought him such delusions, he didn't care. Running his hands through her hair, cupping the back of her head, he kissed her with all the ferocity in him. And the boundaries of the world fell away.

He wandered in a void, formless in a place of nothingness. Magic shimmered all around them.

He was in Oria's mind, feeling what she'd felt.

"*Be careful, Oria,*" Chuffta warned, that distinctive mind-voice Lonen had only heard at the oasis. "*Don't—*"

She did it anyway. She'd been careful her whole life, not to touch or be touched, to follow the rules, to learn the right way. Control and containment and the serenity of *hwil*. Oria opened herself, giving up all control and becoming porous, permeable, and all that nothing poured in—it burst into a myriad of colors, sounds, smells, tastes, and sensations. The wave crashed over her, severing her from everything.

Plunging into it, she gave herself wholeheartedly, without fear or reservation. The frightened girl she'd been—Lonen had never realized the depths of her insecurity, of her self-loathing, how she'd hated her own fragility, how afraid she'd been of exactly this—all of it fell away like ash, burnt in the fire of that unrelenting crucible of wild magic.

After an eternity of tumbling she emerged, changed by her own will, purified to her core being, forged in flames that became her own.

She stood in a vast glittering cavern of crystal, simmering with volcanic fires, the immense derkesthai dragon king splayed across an enormous stone apron next to a lake of lava. The Great One sat up, green eyes round and bright as Grienon.

"Who are you?" The mind-voice, so clearly not Chuffta's, rolled like thunder and lightning at once.

"I am the Sorceress Oria," she declared, feeling the sing of magic, seeing the streaming currents of it in all the world. "I am Ponen."

"And what shall you do with the power you've seized, Ponen?"

"I will be the balance and set things to right."

"Where will you begin?"

An easy answer. She pulled the sling from her neck, unwrapping the sleeping Chuffta. Back in the world, he seemed to be sleeping, still as death, his consciousness in that other realm they'd wandered. But now her eyes had opened and she saw what she hadn't seen before, how magic of her own making had formed a shell around his mind. Winding it back into herself, she freed him from the cocoon of it.

"Finally!" he said, unfurling like a blossoming flower, spreading his white wings exuberantly, then wincing. *"Ouch.*

What happened to my wings?"

"The wolves bit you," Oria reminded him, grateful joy filling her. *"And I accidentally put you to sleep with my magic. I'm so very sorry, Chuffta."*

He cocked his triangular head, eyes sparkling bright green. *"Have you learned better now?"*

"I think so," she replied, feeling the sheer power surging through her, capable of anything.

"Then heal me!"

She laughed. *"As you wish, brat. Anything else while I'm at it?"*

His head swiveled backward on his neck to look at the derkesthai king, then back to her. *"Can I be* big?"

"Is that what you want?"

"Yes. Oh yes. That and fire. Can I have both?" He fanned his wings in his excitement, talons gripping her arm through the padded sleeve.

"You can have both," she replied gravely.

"There is no going back," the derkesthai king said. **"You cannot grow small again."**

"Oria can't go back, so neither will I. We are partners in this," Chuffta replied solemnly.

"You must always answer to your sorceress," the Great One put in.

"I shall heed and serve her all my days." Chuffta said the words like a vow.

"I wish you many together."

And Oria spun the magic, twisting it through the living body of the winged lizard, giving the fuel to heal, and to grow, grow, grow. Chuffta flew up into the air, his body billowing with iridescent white magic. Oria pulled the magic through her from all places, giving him the nourishment each part of him needed. Until he landed again, as large as any Trom dragon.

"Now," Oria asked, *"will you fly me to Lonen?"*

"I will fly you to the edge of the world and beyond. To the moons and stars."

Oria laughed. *"Lonen first. He needs us."*

"Then we must go!"

"If I am excused, that is?" Oria asked the Great One.

"Yes. You have much to learn still, but you will learn by doing. When in doubt, return to the balance."

"Thank you, for everything."

"Just be worthy, great-granddaughter of my old friend."

She climbed onto Chuffta's back, a clumsy affair that had her giggling at his mental commentary. *"We shall learn this together,"* Chuffta said.

"As with everything, my old friend," she answered with love and gratitude. Lonen felt it in her and lost all jealousy that had pricked him over Oria's close relationship with her Familiar. She had love enough for both of them, and he was a part of both.

When Chuffta took wing, she laughed with a pure joy that ran over Lonen like snowmelt in springtime, and he rained kisses on her upturned face, savoring the velvety texture of her skin, the clean salt taste of his wife.

"Oh, Lonen," she sighed. "It feels so good to touch you."

"Yes, let's spend eternity just like this."

She giggled, a bubbling brook of carefree happiness. "That sounds good. But we have to get you to the Temple before sundown. It's the seventh day, isn't it?" She glanced at her now giant Familiar. "Chuffta says it is. Why are you sitting in this farmhouse—and who were those soldiers?"

He blinked at her in confusion, then looked around them. At the palace guard, watching in terrorized confusion, and Fenive hanging back with the other warrior women, biting back broad smiles, staring at Chuffta with fascinated curiosity. "This is real?"

"Of course!" She laughed. "What did you think?"

He looked from the enormous Chuffta to Oria, vivid and alive, her cheeks pink from the chill, copper eyes sparkling with humor. "I thought this was a delusion," he told her. "None of this can be real."

"It's real," she assured him, "though I imagine it's a bit of a shock and—"

"A shock?" he broke in, incredulous. He seized her by the arms. Solid and real, yes, but... "Oria, I felt you *die*." Just now he'd been inside her memories when she died.

"Oh, no." She frowned, pursing her lips in sympathy. "I'm so sorry. I didn't think of that—but even if I had, it couldn't be helped."

"It... couldn't be helped." He'd nearly sought his own death rather than go on without her.

"I mean," she continued earnestly, sorrow in her eyes, "I can see now that the marriage bond would affect you like that, you would feel it snap and think the worst, but I had to break all those connections to rebuild myself and my magic in a different way, do you understand?"

He did. He'd seen it in her memories. And the marriage bond—it was there again, stronger than ever. Laughing, he drew Oria into his arms, holding her and rocking as the sheer, shuddering relief flowed through him. "We can touch now."

"Yes. I control the flow of magic into me, so we can touch." She laid her palms against his cheeks, caressing his skin, eyes half-closed as she savored it. "You feel so good. All I want is to touch you."

"I want to take you to bed." He turned, intent on taking her into the farmhouse to do exactly that.

"Not now." She pulled back, laughing. "I want that, too, but we have to get you to Arill's Temple. What was going on here?"

He struggled to think past the overwhelming desire, the need to finally have her in every way. "It doesn't matter now," he told her. "Nolan sent these men to detain me, to keep me from reaching the temple in time."

Oria made a wry face. "I'm not a bit surprised. How did they manage to capture you, though?"

Because he had been surprised, because he'd simply walked into the trap, never suspecting the kind of political treachery that Oria had grown up understanding. Because he'd been naïve and blindly optimistic.

"Because I was a fool—one who doesn't deserve to be king."

~ 16 ~

ORIA SORTED THROUGH the avalanche of thoughts and emotions coming from Lonen. He meant what he said, difficult as she found that to understand.

"He truly thought you had died," Chuffta observed, sounding chastened. *"Though we got here as fast as we could."*

"Faster than would've been possible otherwise, thanks to you."

He mentally preened. *"I like being big."*

"Good thing, as you're stuck with it. More important and pressing, can you carry Lonen and me both to Arill's Temple?"

"Of course, if he wants to go."

"Chuffta will fly us to Arill's Temple," she told Lonen. Then cocked her head at his stubborn refusal, as clear as if he'd voiced it aloud. "You can't let Nolan win with his conniving."

Lonen set his jaw. "I'm done with giving up what I want for the sake of duty. Let him have the throne. Let the Destrye and Bárans fight each other to the death without us. Let's you and Chuffta and I go find a place to live in peace."

She raised an eyebrow. "Like your mother did?"

Anger flashed in him—so much better than that morose despondency—sparking silver in his granite gaze. "She had her reasons. I understand that about her now." He said it pointedly enough that it would've been clear to Oria he felt she wasn't respecting his own reasons, even if she hadn't sensed the thought, and the insult behind it.

For better or worse, however, she had no patience for his turmoil.

"I just flung myself into the jaws of death to be here for you," she replied evenly. "I faced my deepest fears. I don't know if I can explain how agonizing and difficult that was."

Some of the stony obstinacy faded from his face. "I saw… in your memories, when you kissed me."

"Then what, Lonen?" she asked softly, feathering her fingers over his cheek, his skin a miracle, both velvety and bristling with stubble above the line of his beard. He hadn't shaved for a few days, unkempt from what had to have been a wild ride. Turning his head, he pressed a kiss to her palm, the sensation like a lightning bolt. She let it roll through her, savoring all the exuberance of the force of his personality.

"I think I'm maybe not built for this," he answered her, too quietly for any of their listeners to overhear. "I'm a warrior, not a statesman, not a politician. I never saw this coming, this treachery of Nolan's. I can't understand it now. What else will I be blind to?"

"You'll grow into your power like I'll learn mine. You don't have to understand why a man like Nolan has sunk to the depths he has. You only need to keep your own integrity and beliefs."

He searched her face. "I may not know what those are anymore."

"Look around you, Lonen," she replied very seriously, though she wanted to laugh at the absurdity of him questioning himself like this. "All of these people know you're the rightful king. Even those sent against you know it in their hearts and minds. I feel it in them."

He glanced at the man nearest them, one wearing a uniform she recognized as the kind the palace guard wore. Whatever Lonen saw in the man solidified his resolve. "All right then." He nodded to himself, then speared her with a hot stare. "But you *will* be my queen."

"I will," she vowed. "I am in every way that matters already."

"Watching you walk away from me was the hardest thing I ever did."

"It was the hardest thing I ever did." She let the smile break through. "Which makes everything we do from now on easier than that, yes?"

"Look at who's become the sunny optimist," he mock grumbled.

"Yes." She pulled his head down for a long, steaming kiss. "I believe now."

"A miracle," he observed, deep voice murmuring against her lips.

"I sense the hand of Arill in this," she replied, only teasing a little. "Let's go claim the throne."

THE THREE OF them—they strapped the half-conscious Alyx onto Chuffta's back—arrived at Arill's Temple as the sun lowered toward the horizon. With little time to spare, and since they had a dragon to bring them, they decided to go as directly as possible. Which meant entering from the roof. Chuffta assured Oria that the great tree the temple had been built on and around could withstand his weight. As he'd explored far more than she had, she took his word for it.

Oria had barely glimpsed Arill City in the past. She'd arrived unconscious, been confined to a sickbed, caught glimpses from windows heavily covered against the winter chill—and then what little she'd been able to see in the pre-dawn dark when Lonen had spirited them out only seven days before.

Arriving on dragonback gave all the perspective she could want. If they'd had more time—and if they hadn't had the severely injured Alyx with them—she would've asked Chuffta to circle and let them take a long leisurely look at the Temple, palace, and city.

"Next time," Chuffta said. *"Anytime. We can fly every day and all day. We have all the days now!"*

"Once we wrestle with a few teensy problems like duels and the war with Bára."

"Oh, those," Chuffta replied airily, *"so minor I'd already forgotten."*

She laughed mentally, keeping it between them since the sight of the city and temple had Lonen's emotional aura intensifying with a black and bubbling rage. He had his iron battle-axe unsheathed and in his free hand, his other arm wrapped around her waist. As an occasional sweet counterpoint to his violent fantasies of wielding that axe on his brother in revenge, he'd nuzzle her cheek, kissing her bare skin, or nibbling on her ear.

A very odd combination to experience—and she was only glad that he'd soon be able to give vent to all that anger and free himself of it. As for the passion…

Oh, they'd channel that soon enough, too.

Chuffta flew in over the ragtag outer buildings of the impromptu city. Before the war with Bára, before the Bárans had plagued the countryside of Dru with the unstoppable golems, the Destrye had lived in widely scattered small communities.

Only the Temple of Arill and the palace, which had begun as a fortress, had been in this place. As the Destrye abandoned their homes and farms, they had fled to the protection of their king and their goddess, building ramshackle shelters in a growing circle around the temple and fortress. With the moat encircling the area, the people ran out of room and so began building up.

Wide and full of wooden spikes, the dry moat had served as a barrier against the golems crossing. On the inside edge, the wooden buildings began, a jumbled pile of scavenged wood built in and around the trees. Ladders gave access to the higher levels, and twisting, shadowed, steep-sided narrow alleys tunneled between. People poured out of these alleys—and doorways and windows and every other opening possible— pointing, screaming, and scrambling in terror.

"They're afraid of me." Chuffta sounded hurt.

"They don't know you're not a Trom dragon," she said aloud for Lonen's benefit. "We have no way of telling them we're friendly. Hopefully they won't shoot him with arrows," she added, worried.

"We had no success using them against the Trom dragons," Lonen replied in a grim tone. "Of all of us, Chuffta has the best chances. We have to hope they won't shoot *us*."

Good point. "Stay as high as possible, Chuffta."

"I will, though the higher branches tend to be smaller and weaker. And you'll have to climb down farther."

The massive and ancient tree that cradled Arill's Temple rose before them, towering over the rest of the forest. The temple itself, a fantastically airy affair of delicate wooden spirals, spun around the trunk. With hammered metal roofs of copper, it blazed in the afternoon light, a haven of peace and beauty. At the base of the tree sat the palace, square and secure. With walls made of massive tree trunks laid on their sides, it made for an impregnable fortress that climbed several stories. The Bridge of Seofe, which Oria had crossed, looking wistfully out of its windows, arced between the two structures.

In summer, the great tree—with leaves bigger than her head—would shade all the area. As it was, the tree's branches snaked bare and black against the wintry sky. The ones lower down were much thicker than the ones nearer the temple itself. Those higher branches indeed seemed much too spindly for Chuffta to land.

"Any preferences?" she asked Lonen.

He scowled at the rapidly approaching set of possible, and unlikely, landing sites. "As close as you can to that terrace, Chuffta man." He pointed and Oria visualized it for her Familiar. "And pray to Arill the branch will hold."

Chuffta slowed, backwinging a bit. *"This was easier when I was smaller,"* he commented.

"You're the one who wanted to be big," she reminded him, deciding not to look down at how far they could fall if this went wrong.

"Yes, and our lives were easier when we still lived in the tower, people brought us food, and we played all day."

"Oh, is that how you remember it?" she replied drily. *"Watch out for—"* She winced as Chuffta's wing tip clipped a branch, broke it off and sent it crashing down on the shining copper roofs, along with more branches it tore off as it fell. The people who'd started to pour out onto the terrace Lonen had picked all ran back inside.

"Sorry," Chuffta said, sounding chagrined.

"Accidents happen," she said aloud.

"With the side benefit of scaring our welcoming reception," Lonen added with vicious satisfaction.

Wings open for balance, Chuffta lightly perched on a thick

branch not attached to any parts of the temple. It creaked ominously. *"I think you should hurry."*

Lonen hadn't needed any urging. He'd sheathed his axe, untied Alyx and was already moving with the unconscious woman over his shoulder as he nimbly climbed down Chuffta's helpfully extended leg. "Stay there," he called to Oria. "I'll come back for you."

She hadn't grown up in the forests of Dru, and couldn't climb a dragon's leg like a tree, but Oria had her own resources. Summoning magic from the living forest, she pulled it into herself and created a cloud of energy between her and the nearby terrace. She floated slowly so she could concentrate on not fumbling the maneuver—particularly when she needed to focus on not being tumbled midair by the gust of Chuffta's departure—which gave Lonen time to hand Alyx over to the healers.

He'd been certain they would observe that much of a truce, accepting the wounded warrior, but palace guards now filled the terrace. With Chuffta's departure, they gained confidence, pointing weapons at Lonen and surrounding him. He'd drawn his battle-axe, holding it two-handed, legs braced widely.

They all gaped when Oria landed light as a jewelbird beside him.

"Nice trick," he muttered from the side of his mouth.

"Thank you." She beamed at him, delighted it had worked so well.

"Though I told you to stay put." A commotion at the back of the ring of guards had the mass of them shifting.

"I was afraid the branch would break and I'd fall." She traded him an angelic smile for his blackly disbelieving growl, but didn't object when he stepped forward slightly, positioning himself between her and whoever approached down the widening aisle in the mass of guards. It gave her the opportunity to drawn on the magic of the forest, replenishing what she'd used and pooling a reserve for the battle to come.

As she'd felt with the fallen leaf her first time in Arill City, the living green magic of the trees filtered in like summer sun through a verdant canopy, sweet and gently warming.

A trio of people approached, Nolan at the leading point of their triangle. The head goose in their fast-traveling vee, Oria thought irreverently.

"Geese bite hard," Chuffta reminded her, sending her images of him playing chase with the irascible flocks of geese that stopped near Bára on their way to other places.

"True." And Nolan looked ready to bite. He wore the Crown of Dru, the wreath of hammered gold leaves that Lonen had left in the palace for safekeeping, and carried their father's sword. Lonen had never cared for the sword, preferring his trusty battle-axe. Or perhaps because he'd had to take it from King Archimago's crushed and still warm hand. Nolan's piercing blue gaze sliced over them like the glittering edge of the unsheathed sword, his mouth grim over his neat and glossy black beard, his fury as honed and lethal.

At his left hand, acting as Nolan's second, their younger brother Arnon kept pace. Oria had always liked Arnon, whose well-trained intelligence had designed the aqueducts and whose incisive wit had amused her during long dinners. At the moment he looked as if he already mourned his brother's death, and he emanated sodden grief. Though for which brother wasn't certain.

Taller than either of them, Rhiten Robson, in the deep green robes of Arill's acolytes strolled, wild mane of purest white shining like fresh snow. His brows bristled with long white hairs that curled with untamed glee, as did his drooping beard and mustache. As when she'd met him before, his pale blue eyes held lively interest—and of the three, he was the only one not roiling with emotion.

"Seize the deserter!" Nolon thundered before he even reached them. "Imprison the false king who brings dragons and sorcerers down on Dru to destroy us."

The palace guard shifted, some of them moving to obey, others stepping out smartly, pivoting to arrange themselves in a defensive formation. One young man saluted and then bowed. "Your Highness King Lonen. Welcome home."

~ 17 ~

"A LBY." LONEN NODDED, as if he'd expected Alby and his loyal men to appear and do exactly this. Inside him, though, something shifted and settled. He *should* have expected this. Oria had been right to remind him that he wasn't alone in this, no matter how he'd felt. The majority of the Destrye viewed Lonen as their rightful king and Nolan as the usurper.

No amount of unfair play from Nolan changed that. It was why he'd been reduced to conniving. It all came clear in that moment, how much Nolan feared he'd lose.

Nolan clenched his jaw, a mad glitter in his eyes, a desperate tension riding him. Arnon flicked a glance at Nolan, met Lonen's gaze, and shook his head minutely.

"Seize him, I say!" Nolan roared, though his voice lacked resonance, perilously close to a young boy's tantrum.

"A point of order, Prince Nolan," Priest Robson said mildly, holding up a finger and looking—of all things—vaguely amused. "His Highness King Lonen has presented himself to me, Rhiten of Arill, at the consecrated temple of the goddess before seven full days elapsed. He is markedly *not* dead, nor is he a traitor."

"Did you not see the fucking dragon he rode on?" Nolan practically hissed at the priest, then pointed his sword at Oria.

"Or the black magic of the witch accompanying him? He has allied with the enemies of Dru."

Lonen looked around at the gathering, making a show of it. "Nobody looks to be dead, bleeding or burnt to ash. I say Chuffta, the white dragon, and Sorceress Oria are allies to us all. I have returned in strength, to lead the Destrye to victory and prosperity."

The gathered guard cheered, even those previously holding weapons against him. More cheering echoed from inside the temple, and in waves from below as Lonen's words were relayed through the gathering crowd.

"You are not king!" Nolan shouted over them. "I am heir after Ion, by right of birth order and our father's wishes. You have no claim to the throne of Dru. Resign your claim and I'll let you live."

"If I have no claim, how can I resign it?" Lonen asked.

Nolan growled under his breath, an inhuman and incoherent sound, brandishing Archimago's sword. "Fine. Then die, by our father's blade, as Arill judges."

"As Rhiten of Arill, I agree to arbitrate this challenge for the throne of Dru," Robson declared. "Let no one interfere until the goddess sets Her hand on the King of the Destrye."

The assembly all made the sign of Arill, a murmur of excitement running through them as they all withdrew, forming a circle around the terrace.

"As High Priestess of Arill, I also arbitrate." Head healer Talya emerged from the interior, striding forward serenely enough in her green robes, but with her gaze fixed on Lonen— and especially on Oria—with vicious hatred. The smug curve to her mouth told Lonen all he needed to know about how she'd rule in the contest. A very bad development.

"I believe I outrank you, Talya," Queen Vycayla said, gliding serenely from another doorway. His mother had unbound her hair and it streamed over her white robes, trailing over the polished golden wood of the terrace. Talya gaped at her, clearly astonished to see Vycayla.

"Mother!" Arnon gasped. "You're here."

"Hello, Arnon," she replied. "Yes, I've been here for several days, in fact."

"You have no rank, Mother," Nolan sneered. "Go back to your rooms, where I ordered you to remain."

"Nolan," Arnon protested, putting a staying hand on their brother's arm. "Our father, the late King Archimago, never stripped Queen Vycayla of rank. You're wrong to treat her so. Why didn't you tell me our mother had returned?"

Nolan yanked his arm away. "You didn't need to know. Go back to your rooms, Mother, or I'll have you taken there under guard."

"You cannot command me, my wounded son," Vycayla replied, sounding sorrowful.

"I can and do!" he shouted, then scanned the gathering. "Who has betrayed me by releasing her?"

"I did." The healer Baeltya stepped forward and bowed deeply to Lonen. "Welcome home, Your Highness. It's good to see your quest has been rewarded with vigorous allies and a return to robust health."

"Better run, little healer," Nolan ground out, fury contorting his face. "Once I've won the challenge, I'll make you suffer as you can't imagine."

"I've already suffered unimaginably," Baeltya returned evenly. "And I look forward to King Lonen righting those wrongs. Your Highness." Bowing, she retreated.

"The challenge has been offered and accepted," the priest intoned.

"The challenge has been offered and accepted," Vycayla echoed. They arranged themselves on either side of the circle formed by the onlookers.

"Name your seconds," Priest Robson said, nodding to Lonen to declare his first, as current king. "Choose wisely, as you may name only one."

"I name my wife, Sorceress Oria," he announced, then felt shock drain cold through his body when both Robson and Vycayla shook their heads.

"Not your wife, boy. Not until Arill seals the union with Her gentling hand." The priest sounded regretful, but firm on the subject.

Arill curse him, Lonen had forgotten that simple order of things. He supposed he'd envisioned a more honorable sequence of events—one where he and Oria had arrived in plenty of time to reassure everyone he lived, to arrange the wedding, and then meet Nolan's challenge in due course. Lonen had yet to get his mental feet under him after all the turnabouts of fortune.

"I request a delay of the challenge then," he replied. "Queen Vycayla, my esteemed mother, has agreed to sponsor our marriage in Arill's Temple."

"Does the challenger agree to a postponement?" Robson inquired politely.

Nolan's hand flexed on the sword, a broad and relaxed smile filling his face, an echo of who he'd been before he'd returned from Bára a haunted man. "No."

The crowd murmured and Robson nodded as if the decision wouldn't doom Lonen. He could perhaps defeat Nolan, but not both of his brothers combined. Arnon might prefer books and diagrams, but he'd been trained as a warrior as they all had, and tempered in countless battles.

"I can still help," Oria whispered for his ears alone, standing just behind him. "They won't know."

"Arill will know," he replied, with a shake of his head. "You must not interfere in the judgment of the goddess."

She made an impatient sound, no doubt considering his refusal stubbornly superstitious. He didn't care. He wanted there to be no doubt of his right to hold the throne.

"King Lonen will have no second." Priest Robson declared. "Prince Nolan, name your second."

"I name my brother, Prince Arnon!" Nolan declared with an excited grin, and some of the gathering cheered.

"Very well." Robson nodded. "Then—"

"A moment," Arnon said, staring hard at Lonen, then to their mother. He swallowed visibly. "I will not serve."

Nolan spun on him, sword to Arnon's throat. "You traitor."

Arnon didn't flinch, simply stared evenly at Nolan. "Kill me, then. I'd rather die loyal to the rightful king than enable this craziness."

"You dare say this to *me*," Nolan gritted out. "Your own brother."

"This is wrong, Nolan," Arnon said quietly. "You and I both know it. Rescind the challenge and pledge fealty to Lonen as king. He will forgive you, work to redress your complaints." Arnon's gaze went to Lonen, a solemn plea in them. "We need every warrior."

Though it grated in his craw like a broken bone from a bitter meal, Lonen nodded. "Before Arill and the Destrye, I pledge it so."

"I. Will. Not. Yield." Nolan shook with the intensity of his fury, a line of blood appearing across Arnon's throat. Vycayla took a step forward, stopping when Nolan snarled at her, like a wolfhound gone rabid.

"A man who commits fratricide, before so many witnesses, with no just cause, may not bring a challenge against the king," Robson explained, as if teaching a class in Destrye law.

Nolan vibrated in frustration, then pushed Arnon away, so that their brother staggered back, caught by the guards behind him. Spinning to face Lonen, he snaked the sword in a lethal arc, then stilled, ready.

"So, it's just us, baby brother," he said with a malicious smile. "Get your sword."

"You have my sword," Lonen noted.

"You'll have to use another."

"I'll use this." Lonen held his iron battle-axe in both hands, the weight of it solid and reassuring. They had been through years of conflict together, he and that axe.

"You'll be too slow, Lonen," Arnon protested before Robson leveled a quelling glare at him.

"Let no one interfere in any way," Robson announced. "Not by sound or movement. Or magic," he added wryly with a pointed look at Oria. Lonen felt her move back, though she remained a warm glow in his heart.

"You will fight until Arill makes Her will known," Vycayla called. "Let the challenge commence."

Nolan launched at him, lethal as lightning and nearly as fast. Lonen barely brought up his axe in time, shifting just enough that the sword bit into the wooden haft between his hands instead of cleaving off his unprotected fingers. For a moment he and Nolan locked in place, nearly nose to nose, his brother's eyes holding nothing sane or rational. In reflex, he shoved, and Nolan danced away, light on his feet, bringing the sword around quick as a striking tree snake.

Lonen dodged, but slowly, hampered by his heavy fur

cloak. Stupid not to divest himself of it. But too late for regrets. Nolan was all in, the sword slicing again on the back swing, catching Lonen on his weighted leg—a bright pain of first blood.

He'd yet to swing his axe, pressed into defense by his slimmer, more agile brother. Nolan had always been a quick and clever fighter, and now he fought with all the fury of a man without fear or reservation. Pressing his advantage, he harried Lonen with his lighter sword, flurries of strikes and slices making Lonen feel like a lumbering bear, too thick and too slow.

He'd been fighting golems too long, too accustomed to their methodical and patient ways. Nolan fought with alert intelligence, relentless in his determination to take Lonen apart with ten thousand cuts. He closed in and Lonen swung the double-bladed axe, missing by finger lengths that might as well have been leagues, when Nolan seized the opening to drive the sword into Lonen's gut.

Roaring in pained fury—feeling Oria's terror—Lonen jerked the haft of the axe into Nolan's chin, snapping his head back and reversing the power of his sword. Nolan staggered back, momentarily stunned, and Lonen pursued, bringing the battle-axe around in a diagonal that barely sliced Nolan's chest as he pulled back, but that Lonen continued in a smooth arc, down and up and crosswise again, biting into Nolan's primary sword arm.

That arm dangling uselessly, Nolan still wielded the sword with his other hand, smoothly transferring his grip and bringing it around on Lonen's unguarded flank—again slicing the already wounded thigh. Lonen staggered, that leg collapsing under his weight. And his cloak bit into his neck. Nolan stood on it, a manic grin of triumph making his skin as tight and waxy clear as a Trom's. His sword came up from below, spearing into Lonen's stomach, a spike of fire.

But he paused, face suddenly creased in confusion.

And Lonen brought the battle-axe down on Nolan's skull.

Nolan paused a long moment, eyes wide, the black so dilated it looked oily and lightless, the normal blue barely a bright ring around those lifeless pits. Then his eyes rolled back in his head, and he collapsed.

Lonen went down on one knee, aware of the blood pooling around him, but only able to see his brother's blood on the hammered metal leaves of the crown of Dru.

"Your Highness." Priest Robson put a hand on his shoulder, a firm grip. On the other side, his mother laid her hand on the back of his neck, the healing light of Arill streaming in to give him strength. "You are within your rights to take your challenger's life, King Lonen. Arill has blessed your victory and will forgive you."

But would he forgive himself? "I have no wish to take my brother's life." He sought out Arnon's gaze, his younger brother's face pale and strained. "We need every warrior," he added, and Arnon nodded, lips moving in a silent prayer.

Besides, there had been that moment, right at the end, when he'd seen something…*other* in Nolan. "Oria?"

"Yes, love." She was at his side as if she'd materialized there. Perhaps she had, in her newfound powers.

"Can you look into Nolan somehow?"

"What do you mean?" She laid a hand on his face, copper eyes worried. "Let the healers stop your bleeding."

"Yes, let them do it. But, Nolan—is it possible that he's been influenced? Can Báran magic do that?"

Her eyes widened in horrified understanding. "I don't know of anyone who could do that, but after all we've seen, I won't say it's not possible. What makes you think so?"

"There was a moment." He flinched as someone—Baeltya perhaps—pressed a pad against his stomach wound. "After I cut him with the axe, I saw something in his eyes, his face, that reminded me of the Trom. My iron axe," he added on a pained wheeze.

"And iron cleaves magic," Oria realized, and she wisped away.

"Your Highness, lie back," Baeltya said. Then Arnon was beside him, helping him lie back on the terrace. He stared up at the interlacing branches, a black lace against the twilight sky. For a moment he imagined they burst with leaves of spring green, then realized it was Chuffta, head angled so one great green eye stared at him from a long neck craning over the edge of the terrace. His narrow jaw parted in a kind of smile, furnace hot breath wafting over Lonen, dispelling the chill of encroaching night.

"Chuffta, don't frighten everyone," Oria tsked, wedging her way through the working healers to feather gentle fingers over Lonen's face. "You're right. Nolan had some kind of spell in him. Maybe a long-distance working of the sort that powers the golems. The iron interrupted it, but I'll have to study it more, see if I can get all of it out of him."

"How did this happen?" Arnon demanded from his vigil on the other side of Lonen's head.

Lonen met Oria's concerned gaze, and she read his thoughts. "Yes, I agree," she said. "It probably happened before Nolan made his way back to Dru. We likely don't have the true story of what happened to him in Bára, during the time he was lost to us."

"But you can fix him," Vycayla said, not a question, very nearly a command.

"I will find a way," Oria answered, steel in her voice. "And all the men who returned with him."

Oh, right. Lonen closed his eyes wearily. "We need to round them up. Arnon has a list. They need to be kept under—"

"We can handle it, Your Highness," Oria interrupted. "*You* will rest and recover, as I'm expecting you to consummate your wedding in fine form."

He forced his eyes open to see her lovely face hovering over his, Chuffta's great visage like a moon behind her. "Excellent incentive," he rasped.

"Good." She kissed him, lips moving against his with unbearable sweetness.

Thank you for reading! I hope you loved the continuing adventures of Oria and Lonen—and Chuffta! The final book in the Sorcerous Moons series is *Lonen's Reign*. Discover the epic conclusion to this love story for the ages!

"Loved!!!!"

"A wonderful end to this series. Love it."

"Wonderful end to the series."

"Jeffe Kennedy does fantasy romance right, and I will read every book she puts in this genre. If you are a fan of these types of stories, you can't go wrong with one of her books."

~Bambi Unbridled

I appreciate your help in spreading the word about my books, including telling a friend or leaving a review. Reviews help readers find books! I'd love it if you'd leave a review on your favorite site.

SIGN UP FOR JEFFE KENNEDY'S NEWSLETTER for fun giveaways from Jeffe and other authors. landing.mailerlite.com/webforms/landing/r2y4b9

Turn the page for a short excerpt from *Lonen's Reign*.

~ 1 ~

"JUST A FEW more moments of your patience, Your Highness," the healer Baeltya said, her tone abstracted as she concentrated.

Lonen stared up at the patterned, arched ceiling of Arill's Temple, counting the interweaving strips of wood yet again. There were one thousand and fifty-two in the central spiral. He should be grateful for Arill's magic—and Her dedicated priestesses who devoted themselves to healing—which made convalescence so much faster, if profoundly uncomfortable. Mostly, however, he chafed at the enforced inactivity. Much easier not to get injured in the first place.

At least his mother, who'd initially taken care of the gut wound he'd received from his brother Nolan during their duel, had left the follow-up care to Baeltya. The junior healer didn't lecture him the way Vycayla, as both the dowager queen and his mother, seemed to feel entitled to do. Not only entitled, but compelled.

If he didn't need her help to ensure he and Oria could officially marry with Arill's blessing, according to Destrye law, he'd be tempted to tell his mother to go back to her hermitage already.

The wedding ceremony was a stupid formality, really. With the duel over and Lonen's claim to the throne of Dru secured, he could declare Oria his wife and Queen of the Destrye once and for all. They'd fought hard enough for it. It still stuck in his craw that he'd had to fight his brother for it.

"Try not to twitch, Your Highess," Baeltya said, sounding more emphatic and less vague. "This is a delicate piece."

"I wouldn't want you to meld my intestines to my bladder after all," he commented wryly.

"You laugh, but given the previous state of your intestines, that's not impossible," she replied in a tart tone, her healing magic twisting in parts of his gut he wished he didn't know about. "That final blow could've killed you—likely would've killed a man in less robust condition—so maybe spend this time contemplating your gratitude to Arill for Her healing gifts."

"I'm grateful," he grumbled. Though he'd much rather be with Oria and his mother as they sorted through Nolan's psyche. He couldn't decide if it made him feel better or worse that Nolan's rebellion and treachery might have been fueled by a sorcerous taint from his time in Bára. And Arnon... Lonen didn't know what to make of his younger brother's changeable loyalty. First Arnon had backed Nolan's challenge, then—apparently somehow swayed by their mother Vycayla's return from self-imposed exile—he had refused to act as Nolan's second.

So ironic that they accused Lonen of being enchanted and duped by his sorceress wife to the point they questioned his devotion to Dru, and now Oria was the only person he felt he could fully trust.

He sighed heavily.

"Your Highness..."

"That was a sigh, not a twitch."

She laughed. "I don't envy Oria in managing you if you're

always this difficult."

"She has other ways of managing me than chiding complaints." Which only reminded him that they could touch now. He could finally and truly bed his beautiful sorceress—and he'd instead been laid up for two days recovering. "Will I be well enough to be released after this?"

"In a hurry to leave us? We'll see. Queen Vycayla will have the final word."

"Wonderful," he muttered.

TITLES BY JEFFE KENNEDY

FANTASY ROMANCES

BONDS OF MAGIC
Dark Wizard
Bright Familiar
Grey Magic
Familiar Winter Magic (In Fire of the Frost)

HEIRS OF MAGIC
The Long Night of the Crystalline Moon
(also available in *Under a Winter Sky*)
The Golden Gryphon and the Bear Prince
The Sorceress Queen and the Pirate Rogue
The Dragon's Daughter and the Winter Mage
The Storm Princess and the Raven King (May 2022)

THE FORGOTTEN EMPIRES
The Orchid Throne
The Fiery Crown
The Promised Queen

THE TWELVE KINGDOMS
Negotiation

The Mark of the Tala
The Tears of the Rose
The Talon of the Hawk
Heart's Blood
The Crown of the Queen

THE UNCHARTED REALMS
The Pages of the Mind
The Edge of the Blade
The Snows of Windroven
The Shift of the Tide
The Arrows of the Heart
The Dragons of Summer
The Fate of the Tala
The Lost Princess Returns

THE CHRONICLES OF DASNARIA
Prisoner of the Crown
Exile of the Seas
Warrior of the World

SORCEROUS MOONS
Lonen's War
Oria's Gambit
The Tides of Bára
The Forests of Dru
Oria's Enchantment
Lonen's Reign

A COVENANT OF THORNS
Rogue's Pawn
Rogue's Possession
Rogue's Paradise

BLOOD CURRENCY
Blood Currency

<u>BDSM FAIRYTALE ROMANCE</u>

Petals and Thorns

Thank you for reading!

About Jeffe Kennedy

Jeffe Kennedy is a multi-award-winning and best-selling author of romantic fantasy. She is the current President of the Science Fiction and Fantasy Writers of America (SFWA) and is a member of Romance Writers of America (RWA), and Novelists, Inc. (NINC). She is best known for her RITA® Award-winning novel, *The Pages of the Mind*, the recent trilogy, *The Forgotten Empires*, and the wildly popular, *Dark Wizard*. Jeffe lives in Santa Fe, New Mexico.

Jeffe can be found online at her website: JeffeKennedy.com, on her podcast First Cup of Coffee, every Sunday at the popular SFF Seven blog, on Facebook, on Goodreads, on BookBub, and pretty much constantly on Twitter @Jeffekennedy. She is represented by Sarah Younger of Nancy Yost Literary Agency.

jeffekennedy.com

facebook.com/Author.Jeffe.Kennedy

twitter.com/jeffekennedy

goodreads.com/author/show/1014374.Jeffe_Kennedy

bookbub.com/profile/jeffe-kennedy

Sign up for her newsletter here.

jeffekennedy.com/sign-up-for-my-newsletter

www.ingramcontent.com/pod-product-compliance
Lightning Source LLC
Chambersburg PA
CBHW032220190726
48289CB00007BA/2326